ENOUGH

ENOUGH

A NOVEL BY H.B. GILMOUR

BASED ON THE MOTION PICTURE
WRITTEN BY NICHOLAS KAZAN

POCKET BOOKS
NEW YORK LONDON TORONTO SYDNEY SINGAPORE

This book is a work of fiction. Names, characters, places and incidents are products of the author's imagination or are used fictitiously. Any resemblance to actual events or locales or persons, living or dead, is entirely coincidental.

An *Original* Publication of POCKET BOOKS

POCKET BOOKS, a division of Simon & Schuster, Inc.
1230 Avenue of the Americas, New York, NY 10020

ISBN: 0-7434-5801-X

First Pocket Books printing May 2002

10   9   8   7   6   5   4   3   2   1

POCKET BOOKS and colophon are registered trademarks of Simon & Schuster, Inc.

For information regarding special discounts for bulk purchases, please contact Simon & Schuster Special Sales at 1-800-456-6798 or business@simonandschuster.com

Printed in the U.S.A.

PART ONE

BLISS

HEY

The only thing brutal about the day it began was the glare of California sunshine through the diner windows and the pace of the lunchtime rush at the Red Car.

The counter stools and tufted booths wheezed with customers. Piped-in Muzak battled laughter, shouts of hungry impatience, and the Latino rap of Teddy's kitchen blaster. At the head of the line near the door, a trucker checked in with his wife by cell phone, as three suits—two men and a woman—exchanged lawyer jokes while waiting to be seated.

And Slim performed her manic waitress ballet.

Coffee pot in hand, she bent to freshen a cup, flailed in her apron pockets for packets of Sweet n' Low, twirled to slap down an order and pick up the tomato slices the customer wanted instead of his side of slaw. She spun, swiveled, and ducked, dropped checks onto tabletops and kicked chairs out of her way, all the while singing out, "Hi, can I help you?" "What would you like?" "Hey, Billy." "Take care, Tom." "Need a menu?" "Nice try, bud—does that ever work?" "What can I get you?" "Hey, Rosie." "Comin' right up."

Slim, twenty-three years old, full of curves and verve and a thick bouncing honey-colored ponytail nearly as shiny as her big brown eyes. Proud to be on her own, no matter how lousy the tips. The sociology and psych books she pored over during down time, her only hope chest. Smiling, scrubbing, shrugging, clearing a table, pocketing a tip, she joked with her best friend Ginny who, with two kids at home from two different guys, was considering going to law school in her "spare time."

"Why not?" Ginny demanded, raising a platter to avoid the balding crown of a real-estate agent sitting alone at a booth for four. "My grandfather was a lawyer. Plus, I have a logical mind."

Slim set down a large Coke with lime and, hurrying past Ginny, pointed out, "And you're only like two hundred and ninety-nine thousand short of what you'd need for law school."

"Piece of cake—" Ginny followed Slim to the counter.

"Piece of pie," Slim corrected, cutting a decent wedge of the apple crumb for one of her favorite seniors.

"Piece of ass," Ginny quipped. "So what would you do?"

"I don't know." Slim hedged.

"Liar." Ginny called for Phil, the owner, who was helping the swamped counter man, to hold the nuts on her sundae deluxe.

Slim rolled her eyes. "Okay. I was also thinking. . . I could go back to school full time."

"And quit here? I won't allow it." Ginny drummed her fingers on the counter. "Phil, d'ja hear me? Guy's allergic. No nuts." She turned back to Slim, smiling. "Where you going to get the money?"

With a shrug, Slim laughed. "Blackmail my father. I don't know. Loans. Maybe if I studied to be a shrink. . . " She looked away from Ginny and lowered her voice. "I know it's not cool to say so, but I'd like to contribute something to society, even if—"

"We contribute." Ginny cut her off, taking the sundae from Phil. "We give them food, energy, so they can go out and save Western civilization."

The bell over the front door rang. Three more customers came in. Phil stuck his head between Ginny and Slim. His face was dark, the bristles of his shaven beard white. "Ladies, please," he said in his Syrian-accented English, "Am I paying you?"

"Not that we noticed," Ginny answered. She glanced at the vintage Coca-Cola clock over the counter and groaned. "Oh my God, we've got another hour before the lunch rush is over."

Slim took off with the pie in one hand, two glasses in the other—one a vanilla shake, the other water with a lemon slice—and three menus tucked under her arm.

By two-thirty, the pace had slowed. They were clearing more dishes than they were laying down. Slim piled up a stack of dirty plates for Teddy, the busboy, took a breath, and ambled over to a crumb-ridden booth.

As Ginny brushed back a wayward strand of strawberry blonde hair with the back of her hand, Slim noticed that she had a wet spot under her arm. "Ever try the rock?" she asked, swabbing the table.

Balancing an impressive heap of dishes, Ginny gave her an "Excuse me?" look.

"The deodorant thing," Slim said. "It's salts or something. It comes in like a. . . it looks like some kind of hippie crystal."

"So you're saying I sweat." Ginny slid the dishes toward Teddy.

Slim laughed. "Perspire, Ginny," she amended. "You very lightly. . . uh, perspire."

"I'll remember that," Ginny threatened, as a customer came in. "Your turn, Slim," she said, not even glancing at the latecomer, "I'm sweating too much."

HOW THEY
MET

S lim rolled her eyes, grabbed a menu, and went over to the booth where the new guy was getting settled. The first thing she noticed was that he was carrying a long-stemmed rose, and a book. The second thing, as she handed him a menu, was that he was very handsome.

"Waiting for somebody?" she asked. When he shook his head, she said, "Something to drink?" and tried to catch a glimpse of the book's title as he turned it over in his tanned hands.

"Just water, thanks." The guy had a smile full of dazzling, high-maintenance teeth and blue eyes as sparkling and cold as a mountain stream.

He caught her studying him. She cleared her throat, said, "I'll give you a minute to look over the menu," and started to turn away.

"That's okay," he said, languidly. "I was in yesterday. . . " He leaned forward to read her nametag. "Slim."

She nodded, feeling slightly uncomfortable, and he handed back the menu, holding onto it a beat too long, as he asked, "What's your real name?"

"No," Slim said.

He gave her the smile again. A dentist's dream. "I like it, but don't you think it's kind of negative?"

"No," she said, "I don't tell my name."

He shrugged. Good surfing shoulders. "Okay. Coke and a turkey burger, coleslaw, no fries, couple extra slices of tomato. I write books." He paused as if waiting for her to break into applause. When all she said was "Oh," he added, "You read books?"

Slim half-nodded, half-shrugged.

"What're you reading now?"

She stared at him, wondering what the deal was. Then, just to dull the glare of those teeth, she answered, *"Finnegan's Wake,* by James Joyce. A friend told me it's the hardest book in the English language. Not the *hardest,* hardest, just the hardest one it's actually possible to read, and I figure if I can get through that one, I can do the others."

That did it. His smile wavered. "How long have you been reading it?"

"Six years," Slim snapped. "I'll be back with your TB." She turned sharply and left him blinking at her back.

Ginny was practically panting with anticipation. *Well?* her expression demanded.

"Asshole," Slim muttered.

"Why? What'd he say?"

Slim tore off the guy's order and shoved it over the counter. "He wanted to find out how smart I was, so I told him I was reading the hardest book in the English language."

Ginny shook her head in disbelief. "Hello. Slim. He likes you."

"He's just a dick."

"Slim," Ginny hissed, "he was in here yesterday!"

"I know—"

"And he's back today with a rose." Ginny cut

her off. "He pulls you into conversation. Honey, if you can't tell he likes you, you *need* to study psychology."

"Okay, so he likes me," Slim said. Still, there was something off about the guy.

"Do you like him?" Ginny persisted.

"I don't *know* him."

"What's *that* got to do with it?" Ginny demanded, frustrated. "Slim. He is a *major* piece of cake, piece of pie."

Slim hid a smile. "I didn't notice," she insisted.

"Trust me. Carrot cake. And when a guy like that—cuter than you—he actually likes you. . . "

"He's cuter than me?" Slim fell into their old routine.

Ginny gave her a look that said, *Hello, how obvious is that?* "Hey. Wise up, huh? No one is ever gonna go for you 'cause of your looks," she assured Slim, then broke up.

Slim bit her lip and looked forlorn. "That is bad news," she said soberly. "Because my personality bites."

"Totally," Ginny agreed, rushing off with a tuna melt and a BLT on twelve-grain toast.

Slim wrote up a check for a customer at the counter. When she finished, Rose Man's turkey burger was up. She brought it over to him. "TB, coleslaw, and so forth," she recited, sliding it toward him. "You don't really write books, do you?"

"Nope," he said, not glancing at his food.

"Right," she said, "I don't read *Finnegan's Wake* either."

"I'm going into law," he countered. Then added with an almost bashful grin, "Enforcement."

That was more like it, Slim thought. She nodded. "Who's the rose for?"

The guy shrugged. Over the clanging of plates and conversation, the kitchen bell sounded. One of her orders was up. She started to go. "Enjoy your grub, huh?" she told him.

She was several feet away, thinking, *Enjoy your grub? Ugh. That was brilliant,* when he called, "Hey." She looked over her shoulder at him.

"You," he said.

It took her a second. The rose, he meant. *Nice,* Slim thought, smiling back at him.

The eyes she had thought of as cold now seemed the blue of a warm lagoon. They caught and held her gaze, started to make heat rise in her cheeks.

She barely noticed the man in the booth behind him staring at her. Only when the stranger stood was she able to break those blue eyes' delicious hold on her.

The dark-haired intruder, tall, slim, wearing a baseball cap and a strange sneer on his otherwise attractive face, looked down at Rose Man. "How much did you settle on?" he asked him.

"Excuse me?" Slim's admirer was confused, shaken.

"The bet," the man persisted. "How much is it?"

Stunned, frowning, Slim stepped closer, trying to hear and understand what was going on.

The romantic cop-to-be stared blankly at the towering guy in the next booth, who suddenly sighed, exasperated, and said, "You and your friend, okay? Yesterday. Was it two hundred or five hundred or—"

"What're you saying?" Slim asked. "What do you—"

The guy in the cap turned to her. His face softened with, what—compassion? Pity? "He bet his friend he could get in your pants in less than twelve hours, starting noon today."

Pushing back his turkey burger, knocking the book and flower off the table, Rose Man stood angrily and shoved his accuser. It was either very brave or stupid of him, since the whistle blower was considerably bigger.

"Is this your business?" he demanded. "What

are you, the morals police?" He pushed the tall guy again.

Without warning, the intruder's hand shot out like a snake striking. He grabbed the guy with the good teeth by the collar. And lifted him. And pulled him so close that the brim of his baseball cap cut into the guy's forehead. He held him there, staring, daring, a breath away from losing it, from spinning out of control.

Slowly, the shocked man in his grasp, managed to sputter, "Take it easy, M. . . man. She and I. . . We were just having some fun—"

"Was it two hundred or five?" Slim asked her would-be admirer very calmly. "I want to know what I'm worth."

The question seemed to bring her defender back to his senses. Reluctantly, he dropped his prey.

The romeo who'd claimed to be a writer and then a would-be cop straightened his shirt and did his best to recollect his dignity. Dropping a ten on the table, he looked at Slim. "The bet was two," he said, starting for the door. "But now that I know you? Way too high."

Immediately, the taller man stepped in his path. His words were quiet but they carried the same edgy, almost physical threat he'd displayed a moment before. "Don't come back here, buddy," he said. "Ever." He stepped back just far enough to let the nervous, nodding guy quickly escape out the door, with immense relief.

Slim was leaning against the counter, shaken, with tears in her eyes. The tall guy tugged at his baseball cap and muttered, as he headed for the door, "Sorry to get into your business."

"No," Slim said, trying to smile. "Hey. Thank you."

He nodded and turned to go. Across the room, Ginny was staring at him with her mouth open but mute, for a change.

Slim blurted out, gratefully, "I can't believe you actually said something. . . um?" She didn't know his name.

"Mitch," he told her. He shrugged. "If I'd kept my mouth shut, I'd have felt bad later. Good luck, huh?"

Slim nodded. He ambled out the door, a touch of cowboy in his gait. Ginny started to frantically waggle her eyebrows and toss her head his way, as if to say, *Well?*

Slim didn't get it at first. Ginny's gestures became more urgent: *Come on. What're you waiting for?* She looked toward the door. Finally, Slim followed her gaze.

He was outside, standing there, looking like he was wondering which way to go. He took off his cap and ran his hand through his thick, dark hair. His shoulders were broad; his jacket, brown leather, old, broken in, comfortable. And he was good-looking. Now that the scowling rage had left his face, she could see how handsome he really was.

Slim stared through the window at him, trying to work up her courage. Without even realizing she was doing it, she untied her apron and threw it on the counter. Then, she hurried to the door.

"Mitch?" she called.

He turned, saw her. "Hey," he said, beaming.

TO HAVE AND

TO HOLD

Things moved fast after that. But no one on Slim's side of the aisle thought they'd gone too fast.

It was so clear, so right. And they were so much in love.

According to Ginny, Mitch Hiller hadn't just saved Slim from a creep bent on humiliating her. He'd saved her from all the creeps, freaks, and players in the world. He'd given her an engagement ring only a blind man could've missed, and only a sleaze bag would've ignored. Which satisfied Phil, who was like a father to Slim, of the man's honorable intentions. Mitch had become part of her life, the best part, Slim insisted. He wasn't just in love with her, he was *interested.* He wanted to know all about her, everything.

He couldn't believe she hadn't dated a lot. Someone as gorgeous and funny and sexy as Slim? No way. She laughed and told him again that she'd been busy earning a living and taking care of her mom, who'd died of cancer anyway, a couple of years ago. Her real father? Color him AWOL.

"You mean you're mine, all mine?" Mitch had said. He said it again at their wedding, which was held at his family's sprawling Pasadena estate. He had more than enough family to make up for her lack of one. And while they weren't all thrilled that the girl of Mitch's dreams hadn't graduated from college, much less private school, they were, for the most part, polite about it. And generous. The wedding was a huge, open-handed, if not open-hearted, affair.

"Tell me, Phil," Mitch's mother asked, after the ceremony and the elegant wedding supper were done. "Mitch was rather. . . vague," she said, watching her son and his new bride dancing barefoot, holding each other too closely, too intensely, their eyes locked, as if there were no one else at the party. "Is her father dead, too?"

Phil tore his eyes off Slim and Mitch. Squeezing his wife Salima's hand, he turned to Mrs. Hiller. She was in her late fifties, confident, at ease with her power and family wealth, and likeable, Phil thought, despite her doubts about a waitress's worthiness to marry into her mon-eyed clan. She just didn't know Slim, that was all.

"Her father is dead?" Phil weighed the question. "To her, yes. He left when she is two years old."

"Oh." Mrs. Hiller gave her husband a significant look. He nodded blandly, used to agreeing with everything she said, whether he'd heard it or not. "Well," she continued, "I'm happy to pay for the wedding."

Mr. Hiller seemed to awaken. "Yes," he said. "We're very happy—"

His wife ignored him. "It's a way to build bridges," she confided to Phil. "Not that you can repair. . . " She waved her hand, vaguely. "Repair, well, the damage. . . when there's such a vast body of water—"

"You don't get along with your son?" In his accented English, Phil tried to help her out.

She was startled, but not altogether disapproving of his bluntness. She turned away from Phil and looked out at the happy couple. "He's like my father," she said. "Which means, I suppose, that he'll do very well."

"He does well to get Miss Slim," Phil advised her.

"Yes, he does, doesn't he?" She sighed, not yet completely reassured. "Despite all the superficial. . . differences."

She meant Slim's being a waitress, Phil knew. He was about to reply, when Salima tugged at his hand. With her were Ginny's two children, the seven-year-old daughter dutifully clutching the hand of her five-year-old brother.

Salima nodded toward the floor, not at Slim, but at Ginny and her dance partner. Phil laughed. Ginny was cozily dancing with Joe, an old friend of Slim's who had delighted her by flying in for the wedding. Salima winked at Phil, then bent down and whispered conspiratorially to Ginny's kids.

They whooped in response, and ran out onto the dance floor, tugging at the reserved, so-not-Ginny, Maid of Honor dress Mrs. Hiller had picked out. "Mom, Mom!" Ginny's daughter shrieked, "Can we spend the night at Phil and Salima's house?"

Ginny looked over at her boss's wife, winked gratefully, and bent over to kiss her kids. "Don't eat all their ice cream, huh?" Squealing with pleasure, they ran back to Phil and Salima, while Ginny resumed her dance with Joe. They'd been talking about something funny that had happened between Joe and Slim. "When was this? During college or after?"

"During," Joe said.

"Well, what was wrong with you?" Ginny asked, and when Joe looked puzzled, she leaned in and continued in champagne-blurred secrecy, "I mean, why'd you and Slim break up?"

Joe was twenty-four—older than Slim, younger than Ginny—but there was already about him an air of good guy sincerity that made him seem serious, more mature. "Oh. Well," he said, thinking it over. "I'm terrible in bed."

Flummoxed, Ginny clapped her hand over her mouth to stifle a laugh.

"Plus—" Joe grinned. "I don't know. She had to drop out, money problems, and we just sort of. . . evolved into being friends."

"Evolution?" Ginny whooped. "You were going in the wrong direction, bud."

"That's kind of what I thought," he agreed. "But I guess I was *so pathetic. . .* "

"Why am I not believing this?" she asked rhetorically. She tilted back her head and studied him. "Can I take you home right now?"

"If you've got a sense of humor," Joe deadpanned.

"No, really. My kids are out for the night and—"

"Another thing," he interjected, "I live in Seattle. Women always want the possibility of long-term—"

Ginny put her hand over his mouth now, but gently. "I didn't propose, huh? I just want to have. . . " She studied him. "A brief and completely unsatisfying sexual encounter."

"Hey," Joe said, "I'm your guy."

Ginny pulled him forward into a kiss, and. . . well, he wasn't a bad kisser. She opened one eye and, behind him, saw Slim and Mitch. They were holding each other, hardly moving, swaying close. Slim caught Ginny's eye.

She laughed. *Go for it*, Slim signaled, giving a thumbs up with one hand as she held Mitch with the other.

Slim's big brown eyes looked up at Mitch, searched his sumptuous, intense face.

"You sure you love me?" Slim asked, sounding childish and insecure even to herself.

"Uh-huh," Mitch allowed.

"Forever and ever?" Slim tenderly persisted.

He stopped dancing, swaying, whatever it was they'd been doing, and picked up her chin, and stared directly at her. "You're safe with me, Slim," he said. "You're safe, and it's okay to be happy. We deserve it."

He leaned down and kissed her, softly at first, then with gentle but sensuous intensity. When they broke apart, there was a smattering of applause from the crowd around them, and Phil was standing there, flushed and grinning. "I'm sorry. I must get up five o'clock to buy green beans." He slipped an envelope into Mitch's hand. "In my family, is tradition to give money to groom. You don't need it maybe, but—"

Touched, Slim shook her head. Mitch said, "That's very sweet."

"Thanks for giving me away, okay?" Slim hugged Phil, "You're the best substitute Dad a girl could possibly have."

"No substitute," he insisted, flushing, "I am real thing."

With Mitch looking on, she kissed Phil and he left. They watched him go. Mitch scooped up a flute of champagne from the serving tray of a passing waiter. He took a deep, frosty swallow. Returning the chilled glass to the tray, he stared at Slim. "He really loves you," he said, as if he'd just understood this.

Slim nodded, teary-eyed.

Mitch turned her toward him and slipped his hands inside the top of her dress. She felt his cold fingers on her breasts, felt him teasing them possessively. The sensation knifed through her, leaving her tingling and torn between shame and desire. People were watching them: couples on the dance floor, guests in lawn chairs, even some of the band musicians. His mother turned away from them, linked arms with two of her friends, and strolled back toward the house.

Mitch didn't seem to notice. He pulled Slim tighter to him. "Are you going to give me babies?" he asked, his husky tone half teasing, half serious.

"Oh yeah," Slim said, turning her attention back to him, to his handsome face and strong arms, his brawny body growing aroused against her.

"How soon?" He crushed her to him, wanting no space between them, no room to breathe, or think, or doubt.

"How soon can we get out of here?" Slim asked.

Mitch hoisted her into his arms and carried

her off the floor. Guests parted, applauded, delighted in the grand romantic gesture. Slim felt weak, intoxicated, happy. She lay back in Mitch's incredibly strong, safe arms and banished, for a little while, the familiar, nagging voice that wondered if this was too good to be true.

CONQUERING

HERO

She was four months pregnant when they went house hunting. They didn't call a broker or check the ads. Instead, they cruised around neighborhoods they liked, appraising different styles and sizes of homes. Mitch was drawn to big, spare contemporary spaces with minimal landscaping. Slim checked out cottage and country styles with handsome patios and stone walks and old trees and shrubs, some already flowering in the early spring.

"That's my absolute favorite," Slim decided, as they slowed before a large Spanish-style house, spacious but comfortable looking, with sumptuous, beautifully-landscaped grounds.

Mitch stopped the car. "Nice," he said. "I could live here."

Slim laughed. "There's no For Sale sign," she reminded him.

"No problem." Mitch stroked her hair, her cheek, then climbed out of his car and headed up the walkway leading to the wide front doors.

The man who answered his knock looked to be in his early sixties, white-haired, and vigorous, smiling courteously. "Hello?"

"Hi," Mitch said, forthrightly. "We've been driving around and my wife has completely fallen in love with your house."

The man cocked his head, waited, and finally said, "Yes, it's great, isn't it?"

Mitch smiled, nodded. "We want to buy it."

The man's jaw dropped as Mitch pointed to the car, to Slim who'd gotten out and was stretching her back, leaning against the hood, her belly bulky before her. "My wife wants it for our family," Mitch explained, amiably.

"Oh, no. I'm sorry. I'm afraid not. We're not selling," the white-haired man said politely but firmly.

"Sure you are." Mitch grinned. "Tell you what." He drew an old parking ticket from his pocket and wrote down a number on it, then handed it to the man. "That's the price. Don't worry, it's well over-market."

Stunned, not sure whether to laugh or give in to the sudden fear wrenching his gut, the man looked at the ticket, then up again at Mitch. "You," he said, licking his lips, which had gone dry, "you're out of your mind."

"I know," Mitch agreed, his smile widening, while his eyes pinned the man. "And that's just it. So before you say no again, think how miserable one determined crazy person can make you." His voice lowered sinisterly. "Miserable today, miserable tomorrow, miserable for every single day until the day you sell."

The man took a step back. His robust face paled. His hand, still clutching the brass doorknob of his home, also whitened. He couldn't look at that wolfish grin anymore, nor into Mitch's humorless eyes, so he glanced out at Slim. She smiled at him and shrugged, as if to say, *I told him your house wasn't for sale.*

Mitch realized the man's interest had strayed. He stepped between the homeowner and his view of Slim. "Your kids are grown," he reminded the man, "You'll be happier in a smaller place. Trust me."

• • •

Slim never knew how he'd accomplished it, her fabulous husband. She had felt certain the man hadn't wanted to sell his house but, somehow, Mitch had talked him into it. He always seemed to get what he wanted—especially if it was something she wanted. Now here it was, one month later, and she was packing to move into their incredible new home.

"I told you, you'd be safe with me," he reminded her, as she folded sheets of newspaper around the china Mitch's mother had given them. He was on his way to work, briefcase in hand, looking tall and lean in his stylish dark suit. "I told you that we deserve to be happy. Are you happy, Slim?"

"Very," she confessed, straightening up, stretching, massaging her belly. "I'm happier and fatter than I ever knew it was possible to be. What about you?"

He put his palm on the nape of her neck and drew her to him. "Me? Hey, I'm easy," he whispered, brushing his lips against her cheek. "Making you happy is all it takes." He kissed her softly, then deeper, more possessively, holding her against him with just his hand on her neck. "That's all you have to do, Slim. Stay happy and stay with me."

The moving vans showed up an hour after Mitch left. Slim supervised the loading, then drove over to the new house, and started unpacking boxes. Weeks ago Ginny had volunteered to come over and help. But Slim had forgotten to call her. It had been a while since they'd spoken. Slim had yet to give her their new phone number. Oh, well, she consoled herself, hauling a gallon bottle of Canola oil out of the packing crate Styrofoam peanuts, at least her cell phone number was the same. Ginny would be able to reach her and so would Phil and Salima.

Where had the time gone? It had been too long since she'd seen them. But with doctors appointments, the gym, Mitch's unpredictable schedule, and getting ready to move . . .

Slim stretched to put the bottle of oil up on a pantry shelf.

She couldn't do it. Something inside her swollen stomach stretched then tore like a rubber band pulled too far. Clutching the bottle, she bent over. Her face felt flushed, but the rest of her went suddenly cold and clammy. And then the hand holding the oil seemed to lower involuntarily. The heavy bottle slipped through her fingers, smashing to the floor.

Slim stared at it. Then raised her head slowly, looking for the cordless phone. She dragged herself over to the marble counter where it sat, and climbed, hand over hand, up the legs of a kitchen stool. She began to cry as she speed dialed Mitch's office. She pulled herself onto the stool and stared at the oil spreading across the floor and then at the crimson stain flowing into it; the blood seeping down her leg, darkening her creamy-pale pants.

"Mitchell Hiller Construction," the receptionist's voice chirped.

"It's me, Marcia," Slim murmured in a hoarse whisper, "Will you please just. . . " She was too tired. Her stomach cramped and ached. Blood pooled under the tall stool. "Just tell Mitch I'm sorry, okay?"

BABY LOVE

He promised it wouldn't happen again. But it did. Once more. She miscarried.

He knelt beside her hospital bed and held and rocked her, and promised again that next time she'd be all right. They'd be all right. They'd have their baby, whatever it took, even if she had to spend the whole nine months in bed with special nurses and house-keepers handling everything.

They were going to have, to be, a family.

Mitch promised. Had he ever let her down, he wanted to know. Had there been anything she wanted that he couldn't give her?

She saw his eyes grow moist and heard the outraged determination in his voice.

Slim couldn't disappoint him. So she hid her own tears—tears for the tiny beings she'd lost, for the mother she hadn't been able to save, for her stricken husband, and tears for herself, angry tears, for being stupid, careless, unworthy.

She said, *Yes, Mitch. Yes, of course, it would happen.* He was right. He was always right.

Her next pregnancy was more of a time of terror than joy. The fear of something going wrong tainted every moment. She lived from one doctor's appointment to the next, barely able to breathe until she heard the words, "You're fine, healthy. Everything's coming along well."

And one day, she phoned the construction area.

In his hardhat and Armani suit, Mitch was walking the site of a partially constructed 30-story office building. He was drinking coffee from a paper cup and making small talk with two uniformed cops he'd known for years. When he turned back to the contractor, to iron out some problems about the penthouse, a cell phone went off.

A well-dressed young woman, part of Mitch's team, answered it, and tried to hand it to him. Mitch shook his head and brushed her off.

"It's the hospital," she said. "Your wife—"

He grabbed the phone from her hand and listened intently, then raced toward his car.

Ten minutes later, tearing through the anti-septic corridors, he found Slim. She was lying in bed. Her face was very pale. Sweat beaded her upper lip and cheeks. Mitch leaned down, his face inches from hers.

"You okay? You sure?" he asked, smothering her with kisses.

Behind him, a nurse walked in carrying their baby. She started to hand the infant to Slim but Mitch scrambled up and asked, "Can I hold her?"

Looking at Slim, who smiled faintly and nod-ded, the nurse handed Mitch his child.

He kissed the tiny cotton skullcap covering the baby's head, then danced around the room with his child. "Hey, Gracie," he crooned to the swathed body that fit in the palm of his hand, "Are you my girl? You the one I've been waiting for?"

Gracie. They'd picked out the name a month ago.

Tired, Slim watched through half-closed lids, smiling lazily, adoringly, at Mitch and their daughter, a sight almost unbelievably sweet. The sound of his cell phone startled her. But Mitch kept cooing to the infant, kept dancing, ignoring the intrusive jingle, which stopped after one ring.

Kissing the baby's head over and over, just as he had kissed Slim, and staring into the infant's eyes, he ventured, "She looks just like my baby pictures."

His cell phone rang again, over and over this time. *As if the previous call had been a signal,* Slim found herself thinking. Especially when Mitch didn't answer it.

Juggling the baby with some difficulty, he managed to turn off the phone. But he didn't say anything about it. And he didn't look at Slim.

"Who was that?" she asked, drowsily.

"I don't know. Who cares? Some construction thing, I guess."

She watched him, wanting more, wanting a different, better answer. But Mitch was focused entirely on Gracie. "Isn't she the most beautiful thing you ever saw in your life?" he said, without looking at Slim.

OUR HAPPY FAMILY

It happened very gradually.

Mitch's work kept him out at odd hours. When he got home—often just to shower, change, and leave again for dinner with a client or a conference with his foreman—he'd stop by the nursery to play with his daughter.

Sometimes Gracie allowed him to hold her. Or she'd try bravely to smile when he tossed her in the air. Just as often, she'd balk and reach out her arms to Slim.

"Uh-oh. Is Mommy turning you against me?" Mitch would tease when Gracie cried and wriggled out of his grasp.

Slim would roll her eyes at him, or laugh at the absurdity, or say, "So not funny. She's crazy about you, just like I am. It's just you're a little rough with her sometimes."

Mitch brought Gracie gifts. And gifts for Slim, too. He kept pictures of "his girls" in his wallet and on his office desk. If he was in the neighborhood, he'd sometimes stop by Gracie's daycare, just to say hello to her. It got easier as Gracie got older. She became less frightened and more eager to spend time with him.

But he wasn't always around. And when he was away, hey, for all he knew Slim *was* letting Gracie see her frustration and loneliness. And what if that *did* turn the kid against him?

He'd told Slim it was okay for her to call her friends, have them over. Of course, he had hoped she'd get in with a better crowd than the diner crew he'd rescued her from: lowlife waitresses and guys who could barely speak English. And didn't she take Gracie up to Pasadena every Sunday to see his mother?

It wasn't just people she missed, Slim insisted, it was him. It was them, being a family, doing things together.

Fine. And when they were together, what was the use? Like now, Mitch thought. Slim had wanted them all to have a picnic at the beach. Done. He'd blown off a date—no big deal, no one important. But still, he'd changed his plans just to be with his wife and daughter.

Mitch glanced at them from his beach chair. Slim still looked good. No mistake there. And Gracie, five years old already, cute as a button. But did he really need to be here? They were horsing around together. Giggling, telling secrets, not even looking at him.

Slim turned and caught Mitch watching them. For a second, he looked like a stranger to her, an angry, sulking outsider who was personally offended by her joy. Slim's laughter stuck in her throat. Her smile suddenly felt empty.

"Gracie, want to tell Daddy our secret?" she said, quickly.

"Nuh-uh." Gracie shook her head and giggled mischievously.

Slim turned back to Mitch, ready to shrug and make a joke of it, to include him in their fun. But he had already turned away.

THE MOMENT
YOU KNOW

It was that evening, or the next, that Slim heard the shower running in the master bath off their bedroom. She had just put Gracie to sleep. Through the water-streaked, frosted glass, she saw the gaunt shadow of Mitch, soaping up.

Smiling, Slim watched him for a while, watched the distorted ghost of his lean, muscular body. "Hey," she called to him, stepping out of her slacks, pulling her shirt over her head.

"Hey," Mitch answered.

She was down to her panties. "Should I join you?" she suggested, flirtatiously.

"I'm about to get out," he said.

He said it matter-of-factly, not angrily, not coldly.

"Oh," she said, like a gasp following a slap in the face. There was no reason, Slim told herself, to feel as disappointed as she did. Still, she couldn't help the hurt communicated in her reflexive response.

Slim bit her lip. She was being silly, crazy.

"I have to go back to work," he explained. "I'm showering to wake myself up."

"Oh," she said again, automatically. "Okay." She turned to leave.

"Slim," he called after her. "Sorry."

"Yeah," she murmured to herself, "Me, too." She put on shorts and a T-shirt and left him there, showering. After looking in on Gracie, who was still peacefully sleeping, she felt better. There was proof, living, dazzling proof, that her life was good. She had everything she'd ever wanted, more than she'd dreamed possible. Slim kissed Gracie's smooth, warm forehead, and went downstairs to do the dishes.

There weren't many. She hadn't cooked. The counter was covered with half-empty take-out containers. Slim scraped and stacked the few plates they'd used, then started transferring the leftovers into plastic containers. It reminded her of waitressing, of swabbing tables and counting tips and taking home leftovers.

It seemed like a long time ago, she thought gratefully, a lifetime ago. The disappointment she'd just felt upstairs was nothing compared to all Mitch had given her. She was thinking about how lucky she was when an odd sound reverberated somewhere in the kitchen. A low humming noise rattled against the marble countertop.

Slim glanced over. Lying just a few feet from her, with Mitch's wallet, keys, and cell phone, was his pager. She stared at it as it vibrated. Mitch was upstairs, still in the shower. Should she answer it?

Better not, she decided. Whoever it was would leave a message or call back. But when the pager kept humming, she approached it cautiously, as if it were a bird or bug or something alive. Drying her hands methodically on a dishtowel, she picked it up. The face read: 33.

Slim stared at it, bewildered. Then realized that it was a code. She looked up, listened. The water was still running. Impulsively, she snatched Mitch's cell phone and, not sure exactly what she was doing, pressed RECALL 33.

The phone flashed the word NAME. But instead of a name she saw three asterisks. *** Mystified, she pressed SEND, and put the phone to her ear.

A woman's voice, mischievous, flirtatious, said, "Hi, darling." She had an accent. Italian, French?

Slim's stomach lurched, sending a spurt of bile into her throat. She took a breath, swallowed. "You just paged my husband, right?" she asked, feeling nauseated and dizzy. "Mitch?"

No answer.

"Who are you, what's your name?"

"I'm sorry, I—" the woman began.

"It's too late to deny it," Slim said, calmly, leaning heavily against the kitchen counter, pushing her fist into her roiling stomach. "Tell me your—"

There was a rustle on the other end.

"Don't hang up!" Slim demanded. "Don't be a coward!"

There was silence. Breathing.

"Your name." She felt close to tears. She was almost begging. "That's the least you could do, don't you think?"

"I'm . . . Darcelle," the woman answered, her accent clear and strong now. She was French.

Slim was so startled she might not have been

able to speak even if the woman hadn't hung up. She was almost relieved to hear the dial tone. She shook her head as she stared at the phone, trying to wake herself from a nightmare. Slowly, automatically, she pressed OFF.

The business meetings. The dinners. The drinks. Darcelle?

Mitch, who loved her, who told her he did, who showered her with gifts and bragged about how bright and beautiful their daughter was . . .

What had happened?

Slim scanned the kitchen, looking at the gleaming appliances and dirty dishes, the food containers, Mitch's keys on the counter, a toy of Gracie's on the floor. The everyday objects seemed odd, out of place. It was as if she had wandered into someone else's house. She reached down to pick up the discarded toy, but instead of the toy moving up, her body moved down. She slumped to the floor. And sat there, staring at nothing.

When he came downstairs, freshly dressed, his face shining, scented with aftershave, Mitch found her there, her back against the counter, her head bowed. "Hey," he called, confounded.

Slim said nothing.

Mitch approached her, cautiously, quietly. He

saw the cell phone in her hand, his phone, and one of Gracie's toys.

With effort, Slim raised her head. "She paged you," she said, studying his dark eyes.

He didn't blink. "Who?"

"Number 33. Darcelle."

She watched him, waited. He said nothing. He stared at her silently.

"I guess you're late, huh?" she said. This time, when he didn't answer, she felt the burning in her gut again and clutched her stomach and surrendered. "Wow," she whispered, stunned.

She didn't know what to expect then—maybe that he'd walk out, or shout at her, or deny it. Never that he'd sit down next to her on the floor, in his clean clothes and wet hair, smelling of the aftershave that reminded her of his hard, warm body, naked, beside hers in bed.

"Is she French?" Slim said, to purge her sudden, sickening desire.

"She isn't important," Mitch declared.

"No."

"You're important," he insisted.

"Yes," Slim agreed.

"And Gracie."

She threw back her head, knowing it would

hit the cupboard behind them. She needed to feel the sting, to wake up.

"I must be brain dead," she muttered. "I must be the biggest moron on the planet. Because, you know what? I thought we were happy. I used to think we were so . . . *lucky*. I thought, in bed, we were still . . . " She couldn't go on. She started to cry.

Mitch took her hand. She pulled it away. "Please, Slim. Don't," he pleaded. He tried to lift her face toward him. She bristled again, angrily turning away. Finally, he took her into his two arms and held her against him, and whispered, "Shhhh, it's all right. It'll be all right."

"You said I was safe with you!" she shouted against his chest.

He hugged her, rocked back and forth with her in his arms. "You are, Slim. You are. I promise. I'm sorry. I'm so sorry," he crooned, clasping her, lulling her. "Everything's going to be okay."

• • •

Slim couldn't stop thinking about it. Weeks later, driving to the supermarket with Gracie seat-belted behind her singing "The Farmer in the Dell" along with the car CD, Slim would suddenly remember the woman's voice. Darcelle. The number 33.

Or in the kitchen, seeing the counter where his pager and keys had sat, where she'd sunk to the floor clutching Gracie's toy, she'd think about the moment Mitch "admitted" it. Admitted it by not saying, "You're wrong." "It must've been a wrong number." "There's nothing going on."

Or when she took Gracie to Mitch's mom's house on Saturdays, and Mrs. Hiller would steal glances at her and ask, not quite casually, without actually looking at Slim, "How is everything? Is Mitch behaving himself?"

Sometimes Slim would pass a mirror and catch an expression on her face that reminded her of her mother. A tired, worried frown. A look that said, "What did I do wrong?"

Worst of all were the moments she'd look at Gracie and see herself: the daughter of a man who needed all women to adore him, except the ones who did. Of course, she was being silly there. Slim's father, whom she hadn't seen in ages, who had no interest whatsoever in knowing her, was nothing like Mitch. Mitch loved Gracie, knew her, cared about every aspect of his daughter's life.

When she remembered, when she thought about that awful moment, Slim tried to balance it out by thinking about all the wonderful things about Mitch. There were so many. His vulnerability. It was real—the strange loneliness beneath his confident pose. His schoolboyish eagerness to please her. Why was it she thought of that first? Was she shallow because she loved the way he looked, how tall and strong he was, how small and safe she felt in his arms?

"Hey!" Mitch came into the kitchen, holding his briefcase and suit jacket, his tie loosened. Slim hadn't heard the garage door open.

"Hey, yourself," she said, happy to see him, to let go of her fretful thoughts. Gracie was upstairs, already asleep. Wiping her hands, Slim turned to her handsome husband. "Long day?"

"Come here," he said, opening his arms.

She stepped into them, received his warm, hard hug. She breathed deeply in his embrace, wanting to inhale the scent of him, then bristled. "I smell her," she said, unable to move, still in his arms but stiff now as a stunned deer.

Mitch stepped back. "What?" he asked.

She couldn't look at him. She stared at her feet, at the dizzying floor tiles. "Her perfume. Darcelle or whoever."

"Slim." He seemed annoyed. "We just had a drink."

"Stop it!" she shouted, surprising herself as much as Mitch. Moving away, gripping the edge of the counter behind her, she faced him finally. "You're caught," she said, bitterly. "I've caught you, okay? And you're not going to talk yourself out of it."

Mitch shook his head as if he didn't understand her. Then slowly his expression changed to one that said she didn't understand him. Because if she did, she wouldn't be acting like this, shouting at him, saying she'd "caught" him. Oh, no. She didn't get it. He watched her coldly, waiting.

"How many, Mitch?" she was demanding. "How many are there? How many have there been?"

Without expression or emotion, he answered, "What does it matter?"

It took Slim a second to be sure she'd heard right. At first she couldn't believe it because of how casually Mitch had said it.

He continued staring at her, looking her directly in the eye, wanting to be sure she understood this time. "It's not that our sex life isn't good, it's great," he explained without passion. "But I'm a man, Slim. With the pregnancies, and Gracie, you don't always have time and energy like you used to. And I understand that. I do."

His voice had lost its robotic tone. He was trying to explain now, sincerely, almost delicately, as if he were lecturing a young student on a logical but complex principle of science. "Men and women have different needs, and that's okay," Mitch told her. "Darcelle is willing to take care of it. And maybe that's better for everybody—"

"Especially you," Slim broke in, more amazed than angry.

Mitch shrugged.

"You have a good deal, don't you?" she went on. "I take care of your daughter and your home, and you go out and fool around?"

He stiffened, clearly not liking her tone. His eyes were quizzical and cold again, as if he were wondering how far she would really go with this.

His composure infuriated her. "I don't think so," she declared. "Not anymore, Mitch. The fun is over."

"You're too loud," he whispered. "Calm down, Slim—"

She crossed the space between them in one step, her hands balled into fists at her side. "I'm not doing this anymore!" she screamed at him, her face inches from his. "Just take it? No!

Sorry! I love you, yeah, but I'm not your door-mat, okay?! I'm your *wife.* I'm your wife, and you can't do this! You can't do this to me!"

SMACK.

With the same speed he'd used on the creep in the diner, Mitch's hand shot out, striking her across the cheek. His face was hard, his eyes harder. *Stop it, now,* they silently commanded.

Slim reeled back in shock. Caught between confusion and outrage, she touched her sting-ing cheek where his calloused hand had landed, and gaped up at him.

"What?" Mitch asked. He read her expression and seemed amused. "I can't hit you?"

Low and strong, she growled, "No. You can't."

This time he punched her, knocking her to the ground. Slim fell onto her back and glared up at him. He was standing over her like a boxer, waiting, poised to strike again. He saw the rage flare across her face.

"You want to fight?" he challenged, per-plexed but ready. "I'm a *man,* honey. Don't you get it? It's no contest."

Slim didn't answer. She watched him cau-tiously, but something blazed in her dark eyes, a defiance that said, *Oh, yeah?*

"You have to understand, Slim. I thought you did," Mitch said, disappointed. "I make the money here. So I set the rules, right? It's my rules."

He waited for Slim to respond, but she was silent.

"You with me? It's my rules."

"It's your rules," she finally conceded.

He was pleased. "Yeah. That's it."

Slim kept her voice meek, inoffensive. "But. . . I mean, what if I don't like them, the rules?"

"If you don't *like* them!" He smiled, as if that was the most childish thing he'd ever heard, as though he couldn't believe his ears.

Slim nodded, cautiously.

"Come on. Life isn't *only* stuff we like. We take the good with the bad, right? That's what life is, what marriage is. So maybe, for you, today is a bad day. Tomorrow may be great."

He seemed to be waiting for her to say something. "Tomorrow *will* be great," Slim repeated, with a hint of defiance.

"That's right. Today is the price you pay for having such a good life." Mitch was glad that she was coming around. "Okay, now. I'm going out, Slim. Okay?"

She said nothing.

"Hey, come on. This is going to be better, don't you think?"

Better? Slim couldn't process the absurdity of

his statement. Did he expect her to agree with him, assure him that his getting laid outside their home was going to strengthen their marriage somehow?

"I mean, I don't have to sneak around, pretend I'm going to work. I can just say, 'Hey, I'm going to Darcelle's. I'll be back in a few hours.'"

Looking proud of himself, relieved that it was all out in the open, he bent down and kissed Slim's head. Her skin crawled at his touch. It was all she could do not to shudder.

He took a step toward the door, then remembered something and turned back to the counter where her purse lay. "Just for tonight," Mitch said, as he rifled though the bag, taking out her keys and her driver's license. Pocketing them, he explained, "So you don't do anything you'll regret later."

Then he left.

Slim's panting expired in a ragged sob. Slowly, she struggled up. Though Mitch had punched her face, every part of her body ached. She halted on her knees, one hand on the counter top, and listened for his car.

When she heard it start, she pulled herself painfully to her feet and leaned on the counter. Staring at the phone, Slim swallowed. All her pride, her hope, seemed to have turned to dust.

Her mouth was dry, her throat raw from scream-ing. She tried to quiet her confusion and force her addled mind to think.

Finally, with shaking hands, she began to dial.

A loud rap at the window made her drop the phone. Slim whirled, terrified. Mitch was staring in at her. But he didn't look angry now. Behind him, she could see his idling Mercedes convert-ible, the driver's door open.

He motioned for her to open the window. Slim did. "Who are you calling?" he asked, with-out suspicion or rancor.

"Your mother," Slim said, automatically cov-ering the cheek where he'd hit her. The cheek-bone and an edge of her eye socket were painfully tender.

"What are you going to say?" Mitch asked, sounding idly curious.

She looked down. "I'm supposed to bring Gracie tomorrow. I . . . I'd better cancel."

"Good idea." He nodded dismissively.

"Love is a scary thing, Slim," Mitch declared, toying with a branch of the rhododendron out-side the window. "How powerful it is. What it does to you. Slim, that's what happened here," he explained.

All she could think was *What did he want from her? What was she supposed to say?* Her body was still quivering, still startled by his sudden, insistent rap on the window.

"See, if I think of ever . . . " Mitch began again. He was having a hard time getting it out, whatever it was. "If I . . . Slim, I can't . . . I refuse to live without you." He snapped off the flowering branch.

She believed him. Was that what he wanted to hear? Well, it was true. She believed he was telling her the honest truth now. Not about love, but about himself. About how what he called love could make a person—make him—lose control.

About how Mitch needed her to see him as manly and passionate, instead of cowardly and cruel.

Most of all, she understood the threat he was making. It wasn't that he loved her so much that he couldn't live without her, but that he wanted her to love him *that way*—or else.

But Mitch didn't seem convinced that she knew what he meant. His eyes went cold again. His lips tightened as he fought to gain control of himself. In a calm, icy voice, he said, "I think you understand what I'm saying." For a moment, he met her gaze deliberately, as if to punctuate what he'd said. Then he walked away.

Slim watched him, the stranger in the driveway. When he got into his car, she shut the window.

MORE THAN ENOUGH

The day was heartlessly beautiful. Dappled with buttery sunshine, the green landscape Slim drove through had no patience for sorrow; birds and insects and even the warm breeze bristled with more important business.

Slim touched her cheek. It was still tender, and now looked far worse than it felt. She'd had to tell Gracie, who'd announced it to her babysitter the minute the poor woman stepped into their house that morning, that silly mommy had slipped and hit her head.

Was that what Slim was going to tell Mrs. Hiller? She had no idea why she'd phoned Mitch's mom and told her she was coming over; no fixed idea of what she'd say or do. She just wanted to drive, to move, to think.

She remembered Ginny once saying, when Slim was lolling in melancholy at the diner one day, "Hey, girl. Put your brooding on the back burner. You can't think with a broken brain."

Slim smiled at the thought, then winced as pain stabbed from her bruised cheekbone to her eye socket, which was swollen purple.

She hadn't done much productive thinking by the time she pulled up to the gate, punched in the security code, and drove up the long driveway to the Hiller estate—Mitch's child-hood home, with its lavish gardens and flawless grounds. Slim pulled her kerchief forward, covering the side of her face as best she could, and parked beside the Hillers' twin Jaguars.

This was where she and Mitch had been married. Her hand moved automatically to the car door handle, but forgot its purpose a second later and halted, paralyzed. Slim's head dropped and hot tears threatened her vision. She could more distinctly hear than see Mrs.

Hiller burst out of the house, calling, "You're late, you're late. I was worried you wouldn't come!" But when she reached the car and peered inside, her relief and excitement faded. "No Gracie?" she frowned.

Slim couldn't speak. She shook her head.

Mitch's mother sensed that something was wrong, but fretted that saying so might appear gauche to her daughter-in-law, for whom she'd admittedly developed a fondness. "Never mind," she said, covering her disappointment with a gracious, enthusiastic smile. She opened the car door and offered Slim her hand. "Well then, you and I will have a girls' luncheon," she proposed, patting Slim's hand, "and gossip about simply everyone. Come, my dear, there's so much I have. . . "

Taking Mrs. Hiller's hand, Slim stepped out of the car and, without thinking, turned to face her. The kerchief slipped back

Any gossip Mitch's mother had been about to impart now withered on her lips. "Oh my God," she murmured, covering her mouth.

Mrs. Hiller's face revealed a quick and terrible understanding. The strong-willed woman knew at once that her son was responsible for the nasty bruise on Slim's cheek. Immediately, she opened her arms and Slim moved into them gratefully.

"Oh baby. Oh baby, I'm so sorry," Mrs. Hiller chanted softly, holding Slim, rocking her gently. "What did you do?" she whispered, with concern. There was no blame in her tone, only sympathy. "What did you say to him?"

She knew. Mitch's mother knew what had happened. Something had set her son off, and the result was Slim's battered face. "Come inside. We'll talk and have some tea and then call a doctor, a family friend, very discreet."

"I don't need a doctor," Slim said, walking with Mrs. Hiller toward the house, "I just . . . I'm not sure what I need. Or what's best for us, for Gracie—"

"Is she all right?" Her mother in law stiffened. The hand resting on Slim's arm tightened. "He didn't . . . hurt her, did he? I mean, he wouldn't—"

Slim heard the alarm in her question: Mitch's unpredictability and the terrible things he might be capable of.

• • •

After leaving the Hiller estate, Slim drove straight for the Red Car. She parked in her old spot, ran up the back steps and peered through the kitchen door. The lunchtime rush had died down. Ginny shrieked with joy to see her, but grabbed a second look at Slim's face and dragged her to a corner booth.

"What the hell?" she demanded. "No one falls on their eyeball. Who did it? It was Mitch, wasn't it?"

Slim gave an imperceptible nod. Why did she feel so ashamed? It wasn't her fault, was it? She tried to hide her swollen cheek, but the touch of her own hand sent a jolt of pain straight through to her teeth.

She'd asked herself over and over today: had she been too jealous or demanding, too possessive? Could she have behaved differently, better?

And just what would that have looked like? Was she supposed to say, *Sure, I understand, Mitch. You're a big man with big appetites . . . for sex and a punching bag.*

She wondered if her MIA father, Jupiter, the hippy-turned-big-shot venture capitalist, had ever hit her mother? Not that Slim remembered—but then she'd been only two years old when Jupiter split.

"The bastard," Ginny was saying. "You remember when he jumped that guy who was playing you, the creep with the rose? I remember thinking then, the guy's good, but I wouldn't want to get him pissed at me. I also remember thinking," Ginny added, wiping a gritty sprinkling of spilled sugar from the table, "that he was like too good to be true."

"Was that before or after you told me to go after him?" Slim forced a smile.

Tough-talking Ginny folded. "Oh, Slim, God, I'm sorry. What a jerk. I mean, like right, I was the perfect one to give you advice about men—"

"I was kidding," Slim said quickly. "Honest Ginny. Don't worry about it."

The waitress paused a moment.

"They're like land mines," she mused. "Some you trigger the first week, others it's years in. Problem is, you want a *man* man," she said, "meaning his veins gotta run thick with testosterone—which is good. But he can also turn around, no warning, and beat your brains in, too."

Slim nodded. She was glad to be back at the Red Car with Ginny. It felt for a minute like old times, with the afternoon sunlight pouring in the windows, and Phil and Teddy and the boombox boisterous in the kitchen.

"The thing is," she told Ginny, not quite able to look at her, "I'm not this person, a person who marries a man who. . . beats her up."

"God, no. I hear you. Of course not."

"So what do I do?" Slim turned her hands

over, looking at her palms instead of at the diamond Mitch had given her.

"I'm out of the advice business," Ginny answered. "Plus, I can't think of anything smart. I mean, you gotta go to the cops."

"The cops?" Slim stood up, slammed her hands on the table. "God . . . I don't know. The cops? He's the father of my child. I can't put him in jail!" Slim protested. She threw her arms up in despair.

Ginny grimaced. "Fine. I don't know then."

Slim gazed longingly out the window. Her mind ached.

"Look," Ginny sighed. "Either you stick it out like you're in some goddamn country western song. . . or. . . you take the kid."

Slim looked back. She searched Ginny's face.

"Yeah," Ginny said. "Take Gracie and get out."

• • •

Never, Slim thought, driving over to Gracie's pre-school. I'd never have the guts to pull it off. And it wouldn't be fair, would it? Mitch hadn't done anything to Gracie, right? Despite his mother's chilling question, Slim was sure Mitch loved his daughter. And Gracie was wild about him.

She hadn't explained that to Ginny because Ginny was talking about separation or divorce. Something "normal." She hadn't seen Mitch's face when he'd said, *I refuse to live without you, Slim. I think you know what I'm saying.*

Slim pulled up to the school and watched as a group of squealing four-year-old girls ran toward the curb. Gracie was not among them. The girls scurried into the station wagon ahead of her car, and Slim moved up in the pick-up line, hoping her dark glasses would hide her bruise.

Sheila, the pre-school director, waved at her, then jogged over to the car. "Your husband got her," she called.

"What?" Slim asked, hoping she'd misunderstood.

"Gracie was totally psyched," Sheila said, "I told him he should do it more often."

Slim nodded, trying to seem casual as she pulled away, a smile frozen on her face. Her hands had begun to tremble, she noticed, on the way home. She tightened her hold on the steering wheel. Her knuckles were white and her fingers ached by the time she screeched into her driveway.

Mitch's car wasn't there.

Slim raced into the house, which was unsettlingly still and quiet. She rushed from room to room, knowing they were gone, fearing they were gone for good. But nothing had been removed. Gracie's closets were undisturbed. No luggage missing. She scanned the kitchen for a note. There wasn't one. She sensed there wouldn't be.

She dug out her cell phone, punched the first number on her automatic dialer. Mitch's number. Then she pressed SEND. After one ring, she disconnected, just as Darcelle had the night she'd signaled Mitch. And, just as Darcelle must have, Slim immediately pressed RECALL, then SEND.

It worked. It turned her stomach how well it worked. Mitch picked up and in an enticing, playful voice, crooned, "How's my little *croissant?*"

"Wrong bakery, Mitch. It's your loaf of bread," she said. "Where are you?"

"Slim? Oh. Hi," he responded cheerfully. "How's it going?"

"Is Gracie with you? Where are you?"

"At the zoo," Mitch said.

Slim tried to hide both her panic and her rage. She cleared her throat, then asked, "Why didn't you tell me you were going to pick up Gracie?"

"I called you at home, Slim. Left messages—" She glanced at the answering machine. The red light was flashing. Someone had called.

Slim heard a loud squeal. Gracie. "Daddy, daddy, who you talking to?"

"Your mom," Mitch told her.

"Hey, Mom!" Gracie hollered, "The elephants are peeing!"

"She's just a little excited." Mitch chuckled.

"Mitch," Slim said carefully, "When are you coming home?"

"Miss me?" he teased. "What's for dinner? Oh, never mind. We'll just order something in, all right? You must be tired. You've had a very busy day, haven't you?"

There was something beyond sarcasm in his question, something vaguely threatening. He disconnected, leaving her feeling nervous, off-balance, wondering.

•   •   •

Slim fixed the dinner she'd planned for them. Baked chicken, a green salad, and spaghetti for Gracie, who'd become a pasta fanatic, just as Slim had been at her age.

Between gleeful slurps of spaghetti that left her mouth and cheeks splashed with tomato sauce, Gracie was telling Slim about the zoo. Mitch coached her, reminding her of things she'd left out. Anyone listening, watching, would have thought them the most ordinary of families.

Slim swabbed her daughter's sauce-splotched face with a napkin. Gracie giggled. "You're a mess," Slim said. "Run along and play now, honey."

And then, as Gracie played in the corner of the room, content to lie on the floor with her toys, Mitch resumed the dinner conversation.

"Slim, you made me nervous today."

His tone of voice had changed. Slim picked up on it immediately. She wondered whether Gracie had.

"I get nervous when I can't reach you," he said irritably, oblivious to their daughter's presence. The "Good Father" charade was over.

Slim shrugged.

"I thought you cancelled with my mother," Mitch said.

Her mind scrambled desperately, but she kept her head down, stared at her plate. The sight of food nauseated her now.

"And then you have to go crying to the old gang at the greasy spoon," he taunted. "Whatever happened to privacy?"

Slim's head snapped up. How had he

known where she'd been all day? What was going on?

"I guess it's dead," she swallowed, veiling her panic in as pleasant a voice as she could manage. "Along with chivalry. And fidelity."

Mitch glared at her. When she held his gaze, he smiled, as though he'd been kidding. He leaned across the table toward her and said, very quietly, "Tell me. Do you have any idea how bad things can get?"

Slim was shaking. She clutched the napkin in her lap to steady her hands. "Educate me," she said.

He did, reddening, not wanting to spell it out. "Okay. It's like this, Slim. I'm a determined person. I was determined to have you, and I did. This house . . . the company . . . I am, and always will be, a person who gets what he wants." His voice rose in anger. "And I still want you. You can either accept that. Or fight it. Which way do you want to go?"

She took a breath. "I want to be happy," she whispered.

He wasn't sure he knew what she meant, but he was willing to give her the benefit of the doubt.

"Good," he said in a clipped tone.

Slim looked down and, with sudden shock, saw that Gracie was staring at Mitch, open-mouthed, her little brow furrowed in confusion and distress.

Slim glanced at Mitch to see if he'd noticed Gracie's expression. As far as she could tell, he hadn't. As far as she could tell, he'd forgotten Gracie was there.

How long would it be, Slim wondered, before Gracie was affected by what was happening, before Mitch forgot she was in the room when he hit Slim again?

● ● ●

She couldn't sleep. She couldn't shut off her brain. Mitch's own mother had feared he might have hurt Gracie. She heard Ginny saying, *Take her and get out.* How had Mitch known that she'd visited the diner and his mother's house? Was he following her, having her followed? She remembered the icy dread she'd felt when Sheila told her that Mitch had picked Gracie up . . .

The next morning, Mitch volunteered to drive Gracie to day care.

"I'll save you the trouble," he smirked, bouncing her car keys in his palm.

"Really," Slim said, "it's no trouble."

He shut his fist over her keys. "Then we'll save you the gas, right Gracie? Want Daddy to take you to school?"

Gracie was looking uncertainly from one parent to the other. Slim's heart ached for her. Their daughter might not know what Mitch was doing, but Slim did. He was taking Gracie hostage, making sure Slim wouldn't leave him and that she'd be home whenever he got back. She could always get a car, call a cab, find someone to give her a lift, but he knew she'd go nowhere without Gracie.

Slim knelt beside her daughter. "Won't that be nice?" she said, wanting to make it easier on the perplexed child. "Having Daddy drop you off at school?"

Gracie nodded, plainly relieved. "See you later, sweetie," Slim promised.

She watched Mitch back out of the driveway with Gracie beside him in the front seat. She should have been in a car seat in the back. Slim thought about calling to them, telling Mitch. But even if she could catch him, it would mean another scene, a possible argument. For all she knew, Mitch might resent her telling him what to do and get out of the car and hit her in front of Gracie . . .

Slim paced insanely from one room to the next, not seeing anything, just needing to move, to kill time, to kill the terrible scenarios unraveling in her mind. What if Mitch wasn't taking Gracie to school, but to some hideaway, a place where Slim would never find her? What if he'd only let her see her child if she bought his idea of marriage, if she behaved the way he wanted her to . . .

And then there was the most sickening possibility—that he'd kidnapped their daughter and that she would never see Gracie again.

Slim spent the next interminable twenty minutes looking at her watch, at every clock in every room, waiting. It would take them that long to get to the pre-school center—if that really was where Mitch was taking Gracie. Finally, she called Sheila, the day-care director.

"Sheila, hi, it's Slim—Gracie's mom. I was wondering . . . has my husband dropped her off yet this morning?"

"Gracie?" The director said, in her ever-enthusiastic voice. "Let me see . . . oh yes, she's right over here. . . oh, what a pretty hat, Gracie!"

Yes, Gracie had arrived safe and sound, proudly sporting the new hat her daddy had bought her at the zoo. What a wonderful father she had.

Slim hung up, practically hyperventilating. Was this what life was going to be like from now on? Would she be fearful whenever Gracie was out of her sight or Mitch near enough to attack? Hands shaking, she picked up the receiver again. Mitch might have taken her car keys, but she wasn't about to sit at home.

"I need a cab to the police station."

● ● ●

Slim walked up to the sergeant's desk. She wore dark sunglasses.

"Can I help you?" a chunky officer asked, looking down at her, appraising the patches of discoloration on her cheek and throat and arms.

"Yes. I hope so," Slim said, trying not to succumb to embarrassment or shame. "I . . . I've got a friend whose husband beats her up," she blurted. "She tried to get away from him. He cancelled all her credit cards and froze her bank accounts."

"Well," the cop said patiently, "she should come in here and make a complaint. If she has physical evidence of abuse on her person. . . " He tried to avoid focusing on her bruises. "We'll go out and arrest him."

"But if he's got money, he . . . he could bail himself out, right?" Slim asked, nervously.

"That's true," the sergeant said.

"And then he's free, right? Until it goes to trial."

"*If* it goes to trial," he corrected her. "It's up to the city attorney's office whether to prosecute."

"And if he's got friends on the force," Slim was thinking aloud, "friends in the DA's office . . . " She presented the scenario to the sergeant: "So she comes in here, has him arrested, pisses him off, right, and you're saying there's no guarantee he won't be back on the streets coming after her again?"

"Your friend can get a protection order," he said.

Protection orders. Slim had heard all about them. The women who had filed for them, the men who violated them—violently. There wasn't a talk show or newspaper around that hadn't reported not just on the uselessness of protection orders, but the way they infuriated some men, acting like a red flag to wife-beaters.

"Okay, so we're talking about a piece of paper," she clarified, "a little piece of paper that says he can't come around."

"Right," the cop said, uncomfortable, shifting his weight.

"What kind of 'protection' does it offer? What does she do when he does come around, throw it at him?"

"She calls us," he said.

Slim took a breath, tried to calm down and consider her options. "Is the protection order good for the kid, too?"

"There's a child involved?" the cop asked, as if to say, *oh, well, that's a different story*. "No, no, no. When there's a kid, it's a matter for the family courts. But . . . unless she can prove that he's a danger to the kid, she can't legally bar him access—"

That was all Slim needed to hear. Mitch had the money. He had connections. He had lawyers. She had none of the above. This wasn't going to happen—no way. She turned abruptly and rushed out the door.

"Miss, wait . . . " the officer called after her.

• • •

Slim glanced at her watch. Down at the Red Car, the breakfast crowd would be clearing out and Ginny would be starting to set up for lunch. She took a deep breath, and phoned the diner.

IN THE STILL
OF THE
NIGHT

When Mitch didn't show up on time, the school phoned Slim and arranged for one of the mothers who lived nearby to drop Gracie off at home. It had been a peaceful evening; a spaghetti and ice cream evening without Mitch. Then Slim led Gracie upstairs to play a brand new game called "My Favorite Things." They searched Gracie's room for the toys and clothing she loved best, and then eliminated anything that wouldn't fit into one gym bag and a backpack.

Mitch was still not home when they finished. "Okay, now me," Slim offered. And they looked through Slim's things and filled a small tote bag with what she called her absolutely-positively-cannot-live-withouts.

Gracie was fast asleep, and Slim pretending to be, when Mitch got in. He dropped down on the edge of the bed and made no effort to be quiet as he undressed. He got under the covers, naked and smelling of alcohol and perfume and sex.

Slim didn't open her eyes until his breathing deepened rhythmically, and she heard the slight hint of a snore. Then she looked at her clock, which read two-fifteen. A moment later, a dove cooed outside.

Slim eased out of bed and quietly went into the bathroom. To anyone beyond the door, it sounded as though she were peeing. She wasn't. Having propped up a bottle to run water into the toilet, Slim was getting dressed. Quickly. Silently.

She peered out of the bathroom to make sure Mitch was still asleep, and closed their bedroom door halfway. She hurried down the hall. In her room, Gracie was so deeply asleep that when Slim lifted the child's arm and let it go, it flopped down like dead weight. Gracie breathed gently. Her sleep-puffed lips, her downy skin, brought a surge of love so intense that it displaced Slim's trembling fear.

She knew she was doing the right thing. From under Gracie's bed, she pulled out the pocketbook she'd hidden there and the bags and knapsack they'd packed earlier.

Just before she lifted Gracie up, Slim hesitated and listened. She heard nothing but the seashell rush of adrenaline sweeping through her own body.

With her child in her arms, and the prized teddy bear Gracie had balked at packing because she couldn't sleep without it, and the backpack and two bags swaying from her shoulders, Slim moved precariously out of her daughter's room.

Silent, terrified, glancing over her shoulder, she made her way through the dark house. She stared at the slightly-open bedroom door. The sound of her own footsteps, the everyday creak of floorboards, even the swoosh of her jeans rubbing as she walked sounded dangerously loud to her.

With nearly every step she took, she glanced behind her, peering into the shadows and seeing no one. At last, she reached the front door. Slim paused, the weight of Gracie warm and solid in her arms, every nerve on edge, all her senses poised to search out danger. *This is it,* she thought, gazing back toward the rooms sheathed in darkness. *There was her dining room, her beige carpeting, her favorite painting on the wall, her wedding china, her life with Mitch.* She took it all in for one final moment, and gulped. *It was over.*

Goodbye, home sweet home. For the last time, she looked over her shoulder.

There was nothing, no one in the gloom behind her and, before her, from beyond the door, only the strange, comforting call of the dove. Finally, shifting awkwardly to tighten her hold on Gracie, Slim reached for the doorknob.

"And what the *hell* do you think you're doing?" he roared, his voice knifing the silence.

Out of the darkness, Mitch's hand lashed out, clamping her wrist like an iron cuff. He spun her away from the door. His hard hand seized her throat, choking back her outraged cry. Gracie was gone, torn from Slim's arms.

Yanking her hair, Mitch brought Slim to her knees and kicked her contemptuously, all the while holding a sleeping Gracie like a huge rolled blueprint under his arm. Slim felt his foot against her ribs, his hand still tangled in her hair, kicking and dragging her backwards.

• • •

Outside, in the shadow of a tree, the rescuers waited. Phil's van was parked down the road, out of sight. Ginny, wearing the same T-shirt she'd worn to work, hugged herself in the cool night air. "Maybe she didn't hear the signal," Teddy whispered.

"She heard it," Ginny insisted. "She'll be out soon."

Phil stared at the thick, front door, as if he could will himself to see through it. "No. Teddy is right. She could still be slee—"

"She's not asleep, okay?" Ginny cut him off, superstitious. Nothing could go wrong. It was too dangerous. *Nothing will go wrong,* she'd been telling herself over and over since this morning, when Slim called and they'd hatched this crazy plot. "She's coming out any second," Ginny insisted.

Phil nodded, hoping she was right, hoping he wouldn't have to use the baseball bat he was tapping against his leg. What was he, a kid? He was going to run through that door and—do what? Murder someone? He was a businessman, not Mel Gibson. But for Slim, he would. For Slim and her beautiful baby, he would become Mel Gibson.

Teddy was getting nervous. He kept looking over at Ginny who continued to shake her head, no, not yet. He glanced at Phil, who shrugged at him. "I don't know," Phil murmured to the busboy, "Am I a mind reader?"

Ginny shivered, hugged herself tighter, then squinted at her watch. Finally, she told Teddy, "Go ahead. Do it again."

Teddy cupped his hands and cooed like a dove.

"Can she even hear that?" Phil asked. "The doors, the windows, the house is so big. Like a castle."

"Like a prison," Ginny said. "Come on, Slim. Come on, girl."

They waited.

Phil's palm was growing sweaty around the bat. He switched hands, wiped the sweaty one on his old workpants, and said, "We should go in. I think. Now."

"It would be nuts to wake him," Ginny pointed out. "She knows what to do. If anything's wrong, she'll flick the lights . . . right?"

Teddy looked skeptical.

"I don't know," Phil said.

"Cut it out, you two," Ginny urged. "You're making me crazy." Okay, so it wasn't Phil and

Teddy. It was the damn night, how dark and quiet it was in this overpriced neighborhood. Not like where she and the kids lived. Three people crouching under a tree, one of them with a bat or knife or who-knew-what. In her part of town, that would be business as usual. But not here. Too damned quiet.

Then she heard something. Ginny reached out and touched Phil's arm. He jumped. "Listen," she said.

"I hear it," Phil said. "Something. Not now. A second ago. But what it is I don't know."

Teddy stepped forward like a bird dog on alert. Then he shook his head.

Just then, a scream shattered the quiet, an intense horrible slash of sound, cut short by an even more abhorrent silence. "Holy Christ," Ginny mumbled, shaking violently, "Oh, Jesus, no. Slim. Oh, please, God, no."

Phil and Teddy were already running toward the house. Ginny sprinted after them with adrenaline pumped speed. The closer she got, the more the silence inside the house gave way to thuds and groans. A beating. Ginny stopped running, frozen a few feet from the door.

Phil smashed in a window. With Teddy's help, he was climbing through it. Teddy beckoned to

Ginny, waiting to help her inside. The sound of the glass breaking released her from paralysis. Ginny sucked in a mouthful of crisp night air and ran on its fuel toward him.

Once inside, the blanket of quiet descended again. The only sounds were their soft collisions with furniture as they tried to make their way carefully in the dark toward the living room from which the last awful noises had come.

Phil led them, moving warily.

"Another step and you're dead." The voice was Mitch's, cold and utterly convincing. He stepped forward, out of the shadow. Light from the window glinted off his pistol.

Squinting, Ginny made out Gracie sleeping on the sofa behind Mitch. And then, with trembling terror, she saw the body lying at his feet.

Without thinking, stomach churning with nausea, Ginny rushed to the shattered mound that was Slim. Mitch rammed the gun into her head.

"Don't you get it?" he said through clenched teeth. "You broke into my house. It'd be self-defense."

Ginny knelt instantly and felt Slim's pulse. "She's alive," she told Phil.

"It's dark," Mitch said ferociously, still waving

the gun. "I can't see clearly. I can kill you free and clear."

"Sir. We are three people," Phil responded, his voice shaking with panic and barely controlled fury. "Kill us all, you go sure to electric chair."

"I could give a shit," Mitch answered, his own rage mounting. "Get out of my house. Get away from her," he ordered Ginny, who was stroking Slim's head and whispering desperately for her wake up, to say something.

BAM.

A gunshot, muffled by a silencer, splintered a patch of plaster off the wall over Ginny's head. Everyone looked up, looked at Mitch.

Then Slim groaned, animating them again.

"We are happy to leave, sir," Phil recited in his stilted English, "only with Miss Slim and Gracie . . . "

Ginny was trying to help Slim up. She'd managed to get her to her knees when Mitch turned on the light.

". . . and make no mistakes. If you keep them here," Phil continued, blinking in the sudden brightness, "we will go to police, who will arrest you with pleasure."

An amused sneer curled Mitch's lips as he saw the bat in the diner owner's hands. He walked to him, carelessly holding his gun until he was an arm's length away. Then he leaned in, put the gun to Phil's head, and whispered, "I don't want to say this in front of the group, but you're just a rug-head, you know what I mean? Nobody will believe you. You go to the cops, it's her word against mine. They'll find drugs in her bureau, or her car, whatever.

"Trust me on that," he added confidently. "I'll have custody of Gracie by the end of the week."

Phil wasn't buying it. "And if we take them away, you will shoot all four of us?"

Mitch grinned. "That's right."

"Then we die young." Without warning, Phil brushed past him and picked up Gracie. He began speaking softly in the sleeping child's ear, waking her. Gracie looked around, bleary-eyed.

Quickly, Mitch hid his gun from her and cooed, "Hey, baby, you okay? You look tired . . . "

"You are tired, my big girl?" Phil asked as he carried her past Mitch, to the door. Ginny and Teddy had gotten Slim to her feet. They collected Gracie's teddy bear and Slim's purse, and followed Phil.

As the trio moved past him, Mitch leaned forward. "See you soon," he whispered to Slim.

They stepped outside, into the darkness, and got as far as the van, expecting a bullet or some other move of sudden terror from Mitch, but it never came.

As gently as possible, they eased Slim into the car. Ginny took Gracie from Phil's arms and sat up front with the sleepy child, next to Teddy who was driving. In the back, Phil checked Slim's wounds. Everywhere he pressed, Slim winced. When he touched her side, she yelped. "Could be broken rib," he told her.

"At least it's not my face this time," Slim tried to joke. Then, aware of Gracie, she pulled herself up, struggling to sit.

"Where are we going?" Ginny asked.

"Hospital," Phil said.

"I'm fine."

Phil shook his head. "You are not fine—"

Slim squeezed his hand. "Phil, I'm not taking her to the E.R.," she whispered, "She needs to be somewhere safe. Where she can rest for a while."

"My house," Ginny offered.

"He knows where you live," Slim reminded her.

"He knows," Phil pointed out, "where all of us live."

PART TWO

THE

CHASE

YOU CAN
RUN

The drowsy valet parker looked doubtfully at Phil's van as it pulled into the posh driveway of the Biltmore Hotel. His eyes popped as the side door slid open and a beautiful young woman got out, wincing in pain, her hair and clothing in disarray.

The immaculate older man at the check-in desk was equally astonished and wary at the sight of Slim, accompanied by her ragtag crew, limping over to the front desk. He couldn't help peering, inconspicuously, he hoped, at the contents of the wallet she'd taken from her handbag.

Slim rifled for her credit cards. "A single room, please."

The clerk tore his eyes from her wallet and her suspicious entourage, and smiled with practiced patience. "Of course." After a quick computer check, he asked, "Will one queen-sized bed be all right?"

Slim nodded. "It's just me and my daughter." She handed him a Platinum Card.

It was impossible not to notice the bruises on her wrist. . . and at her throat. But he was far too well-mannered to comment on them. Nor did he react to what he saw on his machine. He simply handed back her credit card and said, discreetly, "I'm sorry. Apparently this card is being refused. Would you like to try another?"

Slim stared at the returned card, shaking her head in disgust, and pulled out a handful of fifties.

The next morning, after she and Gracie had breakfasted at the coffee shop, Slim found an ATM. She sensed what would happen a moment before the machine began to beep and the words Invalid Card appeared on the screen. Frustrated, with angry tears threatening, she banged the machine. It promptly closed down, taking her card with it.

She took a cab to the bank. She learned from a frightened teller, who stared at her swollen face and livid bruises, that the funds in her account seemed to be frozen. All she had was the cash left in her wallet, which certainly wouldn't pay for another night at the Biltmore.

By late afternoon, she'd found a cheap motel in Los Angeles where they could stay for a little while. It was a two story square of rooms built around a concrete courtyard. Parting the faded floral curtains, Slim looked out of their second floor window. Behind her the television droned. And Gracie, bubbling over with enthusiasm, declared, "I love motels!"

Slim dropped the curtain and turned back to her daughter. "You do?" she asked, frowning at the Styrofoam containers and other souvenirs of their meal from El Pollo Loco covering the table near the door.

"And hotels, too," Gracie squealed, throwing herself back on the bed. "Mommy, you want to bounce?" Scrambling to her feet on the soft mattress, its cheap springs giving her a good loft, Gracie began to jump up and down.

"Careful, Toots," Slim cautioned as her daughter trampolined on the noisy bed.

The telephone rang. Slim answered it, keeping one eye on Gracie. Between the TV, Gracie's delighted shrieks, and the bad connection, Ginny's voice was a faint, tinny squawk. "Hey, you," she said.

"Hey," Slim responded, then instructed Gracie, "Not too high, okay?" With a tired laugh she told Ginny, "I was talking to Gracie. We're going to watch TV and hit the sack."

"Mom! Look! Look at me," Gracie shouted.

"What about, you know, what we talked about?" Ginny asked.

One eye on Gracie, Slim said, "No, Gin. No shelters. So far she's not . . . tainted by what's happened, and I want to keep it that way."

"Mommy!" Gracie was stretching her arms, her fingers wriggling and reaching. She was trying to touch the ceiling and getting closer with each jump.

"Ginny, can we talk about this tomorrow?" Slim asked.

"Piece of cake," Ginny responded amiably.

"Piece of pie," Slim sighed. "Good night, Gin."

Gracie had allowed herself to flop down onto her side. "Hey. What's tainted?" she asked, as the phone rang again. "Is that like painted, or . . . "

Annoyed by too much going on at once, Slim

turned off the TV and picked up the phone. "I said tomorrow, okay Gin?" she said.

"Not exactly the Biltmore, is it?" Mitch asked.

Slim's hand clenched the receiver, palms beginning to sweat. Just the sound of his voice, smooth and sardonic, was enough to put her nerves on edge. Immediately, subconsciously, she shifted the phone and started gathering up clothes, stuffing them into the suitcases.

"It's the information age, sweetheart," he answered her unspoken question. "You leave a trail everywhere. Especially when your best friend rents your room with her credit card."

"Well I can't get any cash," Slim replied, trying to stall. She grabbed Gracie's shoes, forced them onto her feet. "Someone froze all my accounts."

"We need to talk," Mitch insisted.

"No. We don't," she said.

"Slim, listen to me. If we do this the hard way, you know who'll suffer."

She didn't respond, but hoisted a bag onto her shoulder.

"You don't want Gracie touched or affected by something bad or undesirable. Do you?"

Slim listened. Eyes widening, she looked around, peeked out the window again. Something was very off about the call. She was getting a creepy feeling.

"Tainted, right?" he asked. Slim felt her knees buckle. "That's what tainted means, isn't it?"

Slim slammed the phone down. She scanned the room quickly. Her eyes were drawn to the door to the adjoining room, to the doorknob, which was twisting now. She heard a jangle of keys, a key sliding into the lock.

BANG. Someone was trying to kick in the door!

Oblivious, Gracie had started bouncing again. "Gracie! Gotta go!" Slim grabbed her purse and the other bags, caught Gracie in mid-air, and tore out the sliding door leading to the terrace. BANG. She could hear the lock giving way, the door cracking in the frame.

They were running along the shallow second floor terrace, toward the stairs to the lobby. "What're we doing?" Gracie demanded.

"That place was no good," Slim said, breathlessly. "We had to get out."

Behind them, the sliding door opened and Slim could hear footsteps in pursuit. Mitch's footsteps? Or were they someone else's, someone he'd hired to catch them—

"Why?" Gracie asked.

"Why what?"

"Why that place isn't good."

"I . . . " Slim glanced over her shoulder. It was

Mitch coming after them. He'd left the door open, the door to the room next to theirs. How long had he been in there, listening, knowing every move they made?

"Mom. Come on, Mom. Why do we got to go?"

"I don't know," Slim improvised. "I . . . I saw a snake."

Gracie screamed at the top of her lungs. She was still shrieking, shrieking and giggling and bouncing in Slim's arms, when they raced through the lobby out into the street.

Breathless, Slim looked back. Mitch was heading for the lobby doors. Slim scanned the night street. Just ahead a bus was letting people off. She raced toward it, fumbling under the weight of Gracie and the luggage. "Hold it!" she yelled. "Hold the bus!"

Weaving through the disembarking passengers, she reached the doors just as they were closing and jammed her arm between them.

"Lady, watch out!" the driver hollered, angrily. But something about the child and the wild fear on the woman's face made him relent. He opened the doors. They scrambled up the steps and sat down, as the driver allowed a few more stragglers to climb aboard.

"*Go! Go!*" Slim screamed to the driver, watching with alarm as the latecomers dug in their pockets for change. She could see Mitch running toward the bus, craning his neck to look inside.

Quickly, Slim slouched down, her arms around Gracie, pressing her daughter's overheated little body against her. Out in the night, illuminated by the light inside the bus, she saw Mitch's head bobbing as he raced for the door. Terrified, she shut her eyes and felt herself lurch backwards as the bus moved off with a hiss.

Mitch hadn't made it.

Slim sighed with relief. She stroked Gracie's hair, which was damp with perspiration, and kissed the child's clammy cheeks. Then, shaking and weary, she looked outside and realized she had no idea where the bus and she and Gracie were going.

It didn't matter. Away.

• • •

Far away, Ginny insisted. "Think," she ordered, when Slim phoned her from some godforsaken all-night gas station at the end of the line. "You must know someone who doesn't live in L.A. Someone you could stay with for awhile."

"I will. I'll think. I promise," Slim said, as

Phil's van pulled into the station. "But first Gracie and I need a decent night's sleep."

• • •

"I thought of one place," Slim said in the kitchen of Phil's aunt's house the next morning. Ginny was sitting opposite her at a fancy, gold-leafed table. They were trying to drink the strong, Syrian coffee Phil's cousin had fixed for them.

Ginny winced at the syrupy sweetness of the brew. "Where?"

"Seattle," Slim answered, checking to see whether Ginny remembered.

"Brilliant!" She knew exactly who Slim meant. "Perfect."

"But it won't work. It's too dangerous," Slim said.

"For who?" Ginny demanded. "Excuse me? You got a better plan?"

The truth was Slim didn't. And, yes, the idea would have been perfect if Mitch weren't so volatile and ruthlessly obsessed. Wherever she went, whoever took her in was bound to wind up in the line of fire.

"I can't ask someone to do that for me," Slim said.

"How 'bout we tell 'em the truth and let them decide?" Ginny suggested.

"I don't know," Slim hedged. "I've got to think about it."

While Slim was getting Gracie dressed, Ginny stepped outside and made the call on her cell phone. She reminded Slim's friend who she was and where they'd met and then asked if it would be all right for Slim and her daughter to stay in Seattle for a while.

Teddy drove them to LAX an hour later. While he circled the airport, Phil walked Slim and Gracie inside. And when the airline clerk asked how Slim would like to pay the fare—four hundred and nine dollars round trip—Phil quickly laid a pile of twenties into Slim's hand.

Trying to hold back her tears, she put the bills on the counter. It hurt her pride to take their money. It hurt her heart to leave them. Phil's dark eyes were starting to mist up, too. He hugged Slim abruptly and shoved a couple of magazines at her that he'd brought from home. Clearing his throat, he gave Gracie a pack of gum so her ears would pop, and told her to take good care of her mama. Then he hurried out of the terminal, mumbling something about Teddy probably getting a ticket for waiting in the No Standing zone.

JUST DON'T
CRY

Joe was thrilled to see her, to see them both. "Oh my God, Slim," he said. "I always knew you'd come back to me after college, but not like this!" He laughed, lifting Gracie and spinning her. "I leave you alone for five years, and look what happens?"

"What?" Gracie wanted to know.

"You," Joe told her.

Gracie giggled. "You're silly," she said.

Slim smiled. It seemed like it had been a long

time since she had. Tears sprang to her eyes. "What's wrong?" Joe took her arm and, still holding Gracie, led them out of the airport.

"Nothing," Slim laughed. "That's what scares me."

"Get used to it," he said.

On the way to Joe's car, she told him everything. The beatings, Darcelle, how Mitch had actually fired a gun at Ginny when she'd come to rescue them, how he was tracking them, seemed to know every move they made.

"We'll just be careful," Joe promised, tossing their meager baggage into the back of his car.

He lived in a handsome four-unit building with a basement garage. "I wonder if he's checking everyone I ever knew?" Slim looked around nervously as Joe turned into the sloping driveway.

"Heads down! Watch out!" he shouted.

Slim threw herself over Gracie, crouching away from the car window, her body muffling Gracie's shrieks.

"Pigeon poop!" Joe continued, laughing now. "Ick. They drop it right on your head if you don't duck."

Shaking, furious, Slim sat up and punched his arm.

"I said we'd be careful," he explained.

"You lied!" Gracie accused. "There's no pigeons."

"Ah, but what if there were?" Joe asked her. "What if I wasn't the lookout and a giant pigeon was waiting just outside the garage . . . just waiting for a little girl with the prettiest hair in all Seattle? You gotta believe me, Gracie. When I say, 'Duck,' you hide, okay?"

Gracie looked at her mother for confirmation. Slim nodded, understood now, sorry she'd pounded him. "Nobody's going to poop on us, Toots. Not with Joe around."

On Sunday afternoon, Joe took them to the park a couple of miles from his place. Gracie begged him to push her on the swing, and he did, cheering her on as she pumped her feet and tried to thrust herself higher.

Gracie squealed and giggled. And, between pushes and shouted encouragement, Joe and Slim carried on the conversation they'd been having for two days. "There's only one thing to do . . . kill him," Joe advised in a low voice. Then he shouted, "Whee!" and gave Gracie's swing a careful shove. "I'm almost serious." He glanced at Slim and continued. "He beat you up, did it again and knocked you out. You have witnesses. If he should try it a third time—Up we go!" Joe called to Gracie. "And you should happen to shoot him, I mean—"

"Joe, you're talking about *me*, here—" Slim reminded him. "I don't . . . go around."

"Go around? I'm not saying you 'go around' like some mafia hit-woman—Hold on tight, Gracie!—You have the right of self protection. That's all I'm saying."

Slim stared at him and shook her head. "You know what? Time out. How about we just . . . pretend we're normal? Just for an afternoon?"

"Normal? What's that?" Joe kidded her. "Normal's the setting on a dryer."

Driving back to Joe's house, Slim and Gracie looked out at the Seattle skyline, shimmering in the sunlight. Tired but beaming, Gracie whispered, "Wow. Look, Mom. This place really sparkles."

"Know what they call it?" Joe said, "The Emerald City."

Gracie gasped and searched the glittering panorama. "Isn't that where Dorothy is?"

"No, Toots." Slim turned to look at her daughter. Gracie was in the backseat, smudgy hands pressed against the window, a breeze ruffling her curly hair. "The Emerald City is where Dorothy goes in her dream."

"Oh." Gracie digested the information. "Where is she when she wakes up?"

"Back home in Kansas," Slim explained.

"Careful!" Joe shouted. "Look out! Duck your heads!"

"Quick," Slim played along. "Look out! Pigeon poop!"

As Joe approached his street, Slim and Gracie dropped their heads out of sight. "Quiet," Slim teased, clamping her hand over her squealing daughter's mouth, "if those pigeons hear you laughing at them, uh-oh, are we going to be in trouble."

"Beware," Joe intoned, ominously and, looking as though he were alone in his car, he turned the corner and drove into the basement garage.

• • •

It can't last, Slim thought, watching Joe drying the dinner dishes. She'd bathed Gracie, wrapped her in an old flannel shirt of his, and was combing out her daughter's hair.

"Decaf or high test?" Joe asked, wiping his hands on the drying towel.

"Definitely decaf," Slim said. "Joe, I can't tell you what these past few days have meant to me . . . to us. It's amazing to feel so comfortable and taken care of."

"Yeah, that's me," he teased her, "Seattle's host with the most." He began to prepare the coffee. Over his shoulder he said, casually, "Slim? What made you . . . I mean, why'd you come here, to me?"

It was a good question. She studied him, his back anyway, and saw how his dark brown hair curled over the collar of his denim shirt. She knew how it would feel to run her fingers through that hair, remembered the fragrance and texture of it. And the warmth of his lanky neck and lean shoulders.

He was waiting for her answer. "Actually, I. . . I tried to think of the last time I felt safe. . . and I saw your face. Also," she laughed nervously, "I needed someone M-I-T-C-H wouldn't think of right away."

He turned toward her. "And someone who was stupid enough to do it."

"That, too," Slim admitted, "That was the main consideration."

"That's what I figured," Joe said. "Okay, anybody here like hot fudge sundaes?"

Gracie whooped.

The doorbell rang. Slim and Joe froze, staring at each other. Slim whipped her hand over Gracie's mouth. "Hey, Mom." Gracie looked horrified. "Why'd you—"

Slim put her finger to her mouth. "Shhh, Toots." She took Gracie's hand and they scurried out of sight as Joe rushed to the stereo and put it on, hoping the music would cover Gracie's "whoop."

Through the peephole, Joe saw a stranger, a big, serious looking man who, from the narrow vantage of the peephole, appeared to be wearing a dark suit. The guy looked nothing like a Jehovah's Witness. "Yes?" Joe asked, turning to be sure Slim and Gracie were nowhere to be seen.

"FBI," the man said, holding up an I.D. tag that Joe couldn't read through the peephole. "Can we talk?"

"Sure," Joe said. "Go ahead."

The serious man glanced over his shoulder into the darkness, which was when Joe realized the outside light wasn't working. Facing the peephole again, he said, in a bland, unhurried way, "Would you mind opening up? We're investigating a kidnapping. We'd like to look around."

"Do you have a warrant?" Joe stalled.

With a weary sigh, the FBI agent held up the warrant.

Joe turned again, looking behind him into the apartment where there was no sign that anyone was there but him; even the dinner table was cleared and the dishes out of the way. "Okay," he said, opening the door.

Immediately, the big man and two others in suits pushed brusquely past him. "Can I actually *see* the warrant?" he said, irritably, as the men fanned out, ignoring him. Of the three, one, wearing black-rimmed glasses and a ponytail, was quick and jumpy, his movements more frenzied and violent than the others. "Who are you looking for?" Joe tried again. The jumpy FBI guy glanced at him contemptuously.

Joe walked past him, so that he could see the other agents. The big guy had ducked into the kitchen and was checking out the pantry, moving things out of his way, thumping on walls. Was he looking for a crawl space, a hidden passageway? Joe was almost relieved by the idiocy of the search. Still, it felt like his heart was pounding hard enough for them to hear it over the music—which stopped abruptly as the manic agent knocked over his old stereo.

"Hey." Joe charged back into the living room.

"Oops," the guy said, sarcastically.

The bedroom door was open and the third FBI guy was bent over, checking under the bed. He stood abruptly, opened Joe's closet door and began yanking clothes aside. Panicked, Joe looked at the floor of the closet, expecting to see two pair of feet. Gracie's bear was stuck away on the upper shelf, behind Joe's sweaters.

"Mister, unless you leave right now," he hollered into the one checking out the closet, "I'm calling the police." It was the first thing that came to mind, and stupid, Joe thought.

The nervous guy in the living room agreed. "Oh, jeez," he mocked, "that's a scary thought."

Joe brushed past the man and picked up the phone. The guy tore it out of his hand and slammed it down. "I *married* a cop, okay? I don't need their bullshit right now."

It sounded plausible. But this so-called "investigation" still seemed bogus. They hadn't asked him a single question, and now the big guy had gone down to the garage to check out Joe's car. Was that where they had run? Were Slim and Gracie in his car or under it?

The bedroom searcher came out empty-handed and headed for the kitchen. Joe followed the man's eyes as they scanned the room. And then he saw it, the slightly ajar cabinet door. The bedroom guy looked right past it, but Joe's gaze lingered on the cabinet maybe a second too long. Long enough to know that's where they were.

Now the man was throwing open doors and drawers, methodically making his way toward the cabinet. The third guy, the jumpy one, had moved close to Joe and was watching him malevolently, waiting for him to make a wrong move, daring him to say something.

It didn't matter. The guy in the kitchen was too close to Slim and Gracie.

"That's enough," Joe called, forcefully. "You hear me? It's time to go. Now!"

The crazy guy guarding Joe smiled, as if this was what he'd been hoping for.

"You're not FBI. I know who you are, okay? I know who hired you—"

"Yeah?" Suddenly, there was a knife in the man's hand. He put it to Joe's throat. "You know what it feels like to have a knife hit your carotid?"

"No," Joe said, feeling the blade on his neck, trying not to move. Had he heard Gracie gasp? Had the phony FBI guys heard it?

"You know what it's like to bleed out in less than two minutes?" knife man asked, clearly enjoying himself.

"No, I really don't," Joe answered, his brain addled by wild thoughts. He knew he should be hoping he survived instead of wishing this were taking place out of sight of the cabinet, where Gracie might see it, where Slim might decide to give herself up.

"John Boy's got a brand new shiv," the man in the kitchen laughed, and stopped his search.

"I'm just going to cut him a little—"

"Sure you want the felony?" his partner asked, strolling into the living room.

"I don't mind," the crazy one assured him.

Joe's eyes darted to the cabinet, where he thought he'd seen a movement. More than the knife at his throat, the sight of something, Slim's fingers, he thought, on the cabinet door turned his blood cold. Don't, he ordered her, silently. For God's sake. . .

"John Boy!" The big man, who'd been checking out the garage, burst in. "This is not listed on the program," he warned the guy with the knife. "Come on, they're not here. Let's ride," he said.

There was no time to breath a sigh of relief. Knife man didn't move. "Can't I just cut him a—"

"No! Not today," the big guy commanded. "Let's go."

They headed for the door. "'Night, John Boy," Joe called.

Glaring back at him, the crazy one grinned maliciously and ran his knife along the couch, spilling out its contents, then continued along the wall, leaving a vicious scar in the plaster. Then the door slammed, and they were gone.

The apartment was absolutely silent for a moment. Joe stared at the cabinet. Had he imagined they were in there? Dreamed up the sight of Slim's hand on the door? He waited, listening for their car to leave, then he walked into the kitchen. The cabinet door opened and Slim and Gracie spilled out.

Gracie was crying. Slim hugged her, drew a tissue from her pocket. "You okay?" she asked Joe.

He felt his neck. "I guess. I needed a shave, anyway."

Slim didn't smile. "I shouldn't be here—"

"Sure you should," he said, evenly.

"I can't put people I love in danger," she insisted. He noticed that she was crying, too. Tears welled in her eyes but she ignored them, and continued swabbing Gracie's wet cheeks with the crumpled tissue.

"What danger?" he tried to joke. "They killed my sofa."

The telephone rang and they jumped. Slim, stroking Gracie's hair, looked at Joe, who was staring at the phone. It rang again. Joe went to it. "No," Slim whispered. He glanced at her, then answered the phone.

The moment he said, "Hello," the voice at the other end said, "This is Mitch Hiller, Joe."

"Hello," he responded, "Yes, how are you?" Slim stared at him, waiting. Joe nodded to her, yes, it was Mitch. Then he cocked his head at Gracie, indicating that Slim should take her into the bedroom.

"I assume Slim's called you," Mitch said, in a calm, friendly voice, as Slim led Gracie from the room.

Joe watched them go. Then answered, "Of course."

"Will you give her a message?" he asked, pleasantly. "If she calls again, I mean?"

"I don't know," Joe said, as Slim came back in, alone. She walked directly over to Joe who moved the phone so that she could listen in. "I'm on her side here, not yours."

"Her side?" Mitch hesitated. Joe could hear noise in the background, a crowd cheering, an announcer's voice. Mitch was either watching a basketball game on TV or phoning from courtside. Finally, he said, as if he were wounded by Joe's words but still willing to be gracious, "Come on, Joe, you're a smart guy. Let me say two words, okay? 'Lug nuts.' You don't want to worry they're loose every time you get in your car. And how about the windows to your apartment. Are they still locked? A person could go crazy thinking about stuff like that."

"Goodbye, Mitch," Joe said.

"Tell her to call her friends," Mitch added, ominously, just before he hung up.

Slim froze. "Oh, God, Joe. Did he say my friends?" she asked, alarmed.

● ● ●

The phone rang and rang at the diner. Finally, Ginny ran over and picked it up—more to stop the ringing than to find out who was calling in the middle of this horror show. All attitude, she growled, "Yeah? Phil's."

"Hey, it's me." Slim said.

"Can you believe this?" Ginny shouted, anger barely masking her distress. "This is unbelievable!" She looked over at the entrance, where a hefty man in a suit, and two uniformed policemen were waylaying Phil.

"I am taxpayer!" Phil was shouting, outraged. "Last year I pay nineteen thousand American income tax!"

"What was that?" Slim asked. "Gin, what's going on?"

"Immigration is here!" Ginny wailed. "And the police, two policemen. They claim they can revoke Phil's green card—"

"What?!" Slim was appalled.

Before she could warn Ginny to check their I.D., make sure they were legit, the distraught waitress added, "Breaking into Mitch's house; it's a felony. I called Immigration. They're serious. Worst case, they can deport him—Oh, crap, he's fighting with the cops!"

"Keep hands off me, huh?!" Phil demanded, shoving one of the officers, who'd taken his arm.

"Hey! Phil!" Ginny shouted, practically in tears. "You fight with a cop, you *will* get deported."

"Okay, okay." Phil looked at Ginny and raised his hands in a gesture of surrender. "I am smart, okay?"

"This is all Mitch," Slim said. "All his idea."

"What?!" Ginny asked, distracted.

"This isn't real," Slim tried again. "Think about it. Mitch doesn't want you testifying that he beat me up. He's just trying to scare you so you guys won't help me anymore."

Phil was being led out. "Do not tell my children," he called to Ginny, "Please."

"Oh, God, Phil—"

"Never," he insisted, seeing how she was looking at him, eyes wide with fear and pity. "Never they should have this picture."

Nodding, promising, Ginny tried to pull herself together as the police took Phil out the door.

"Tell him I'm sorry, Gin," Slim urged her.

"Don't worry about it," she said, sounding exhausted. Then with familiar ferocity, she pledged, "We'll take care of it, okay?"

"Okay," Slim responded. "Ginny. . . I'm really, really sorry."

* * *

An hour later, in Joe's apartment, Gracie watched solemnly as her mother, with swift purpose, finished packing up their few belongings.

"You don't have to go," Joe told her again. "You don't have to leave this way, Slim. They won't come back tonight."

"No. No, it's not that," she tried once more to explain. "I'm dangerous, Joe. It's dangerous to know me right now."

"Slim, come on—" He'd already argued that he didn't care, it didn't matter, he could handle it. Now, he said, "Okay. But you can come back anytime, right? Tomorrow, the next day . . . "

"Tomorrow, can we?" Gracie asked, gravely. Slim ruffled her daughter's hair and handed her her teddy bear.

"Thanks." She smiled gratefully at Joe. Then

zipped up the gym bag, shouldered her back-pack, and took Gracie's hand. "Maybe one day we'll take you up on that."

He nodded. "Where are you going to go, Slim? What are you going to do?"

She looked at him, considered for a moment, then touched his cheek. "Thanks, Joe. For everything."

● ● ●

"Mom, tell me again. Where are we?" Gracie, teddy bear under her arm, was walking along-side Slim, gripping her hand, and gazing out at the new Oz they'd come to.

"San Francisco, Toots." Slim was checking street addresses in a renovated warehouse dis-trict south of Market. The neighborhood's old brick factories, with their wide windows and high ceilings, had been converted to "charm-ing"—read: gentrified, trendy, and over-priced—office buildings. But Gracie was staring at the towering glass pyramid in the distance. "That's the TransAmerica building," Slim told her. "And that, over there," she pointed to her quarry, at last, "is where we're going."

The logo on the frosted-glass, top floor door

read, VCVC. Viet Cong Venture Capital, Slim remembered from the article in one of the magazines Phil had given her for the flight to Seattle. The wide door itself was flung open. Inside the spacious, airy, full floor loft, a hive of attractive young people in jeans and long hair were leaning over drawing tables in twos and threes, working on what looked like a hundred different projects. Miniature models of buildings, computer images projected on big screen monitors; music, vibrant bluesy classics, blew from the multi-speakers of a stacked silver modular system.

"Hey." A blonde in a fitted black T-shirt, worn jeans and sandals, noticed Slim and Gracie. "Can I help you?" she asked in a friendly blonde way.

"I'm here to see my father," Slim said.

"And he might be?"

"Jupiter Slakowski," Slim answered, tightly. "Is he around?"

The girl checked her out, smiled, and pointed to a glass block cubicle at the far end of the loft. Through the thick glass, Slim could make out the shadow of a tall, youthful figure. The blonde led Slim over and called into the office, "Hey Jupe. Girl out there. Says she's your daughter." To Slim, she said, "Good luck," and went back to her drawing board.

Jupiter stuck his head out and, silently, looked them up and down. He was better looking than she'd imagined. Not all that different from the single photo of him her mother had kept. Although he had to be in his mid-fifties now. Tall, confident, amused, a skeptical, craggy guy with a single white streak in his glossy dark brown hair. His eyes took her in, then moved on to Gracie.

"She can't be my daughter," he announced. "I haven't had sex in a while . . . Well, not in this country anyway."

"Not her," Slim said, irritably. "Me. I'm your daughter."

The man eyed her again. Impudently, Slim sized him up, too. Finally, he motioned for her to follow him into his office.

On his way to his desk, his broad back to her, he asked nonchalantly, "What year were you born?"

"You are my dad, Jupiter," Slim said, not wanting to go through a paternity Q&A. "I wrote to you, like twenty times, but even when Mom died, you wouldn't answer."

He turned around, still not buying it.

"I didn't have enough money to bury her. That was really fun."

"Hey, don't look at me." With an engaging

smile, Jupiter raised his hands defensively. "I didn't kill her."

"Right," Slim said. "You had help."

He sat down, frowning now. "That's a stupid thing to say. What do you want, money?"

Slim sighed. "I wanted Gracie to meet her Grandpa."

Dutifully, without warmth, he nodded at the child. "Hi."

Gracie looked at him doubtfully.

"And yes," Slim said, "we need money. To survive."

Jupiter laughed. "Look sweetheart. From the late sixties into the seventies, I had five kids, maybe more." He motioned out to the busy loft. "Anyone in that room could be my kid. It's a running joke around here."

"I'm not laughing," Slim said, coldly. Much to her surprise, she wasn't trembling with nerves, or anger either, except for the total lack of interest he'd shown in Gracie. There wasn't time for sentimentality. She hadn't come for a father-daughter reunion. She'd come because she needed help and he was supposed to be smart and had money and was the one person in her life, or at the edge of it, who Mitch didn't know. How could he? She'd barely known him herself. "You want to wake up one day and find out your daughter's dead, and you didn't do anything to help her?"

"Oh, you're good." Jupiter shook his head in mock admiration. "And the kid, that's a nice touch. But it's not exactly original." He leaned across his desk. "You're not the first one to think of this gig. Especially since that article in *Fortune*. So listen," he reached into his back pocket and took out his wallet. "I'll give you the same thing I gave the other three. Six bucks. Enough for a sandwich. Tell you what, sweetheart, for you, it's twelve. Buy the kid a sandwich, too."

Jupiter pushed the money across his desk. Slim stared at it, nodded, and began fiddling with the gold chain around her neck. She removed an antique woman's ring that hung on the chain, and slid it back across the table at him.

Standing, picking Gracie up, she said, "I think that originally belonged to you. If you're so hard up, you can pawn it. It's worth more than twelve dollars."

Turning on her heels, leaving the money untouched, she walked out.

Jupiter shook his head, then picked up the ring, and examined it. Searching his memory, he turned the gold band over in his hand. After a while, smiling regretfully, he murmured, "Man, it's been a long time," and leaned back in his chair as memories came flooding back.

In the alleyway behind Jupiter's building, Slim, still carrying Gracie, stood in the shadows trying to figure out her next move.

"Hey, Mom," Gracie said, her little fingers tenderly raking Slim's cheek. "Don't cry. Okay, Mom? Please don't cry."

Slim snuffled, awkwardly reached in her pocket for a tissue.

"You have *me,*" Gracie promised.

A NEW LEAF

Twenty-four hours later, Slim was a new person.

Courtesy of Phil and Western Union, Slim had traversed half the country by train, airplane, and now, taxicab, all the way to the Great Lakes. After a couple of hours of research, fifteen minutes at the county recorder's desk, two phone calls, and a long, chilly ferry ride, she was Erin Shleeter—a woman with a little girl, a new hairstyle and a new look.

Slim had found the name in a microfiche edition of an old Michigan newspaper death notice: "Erin Shleeter, six weeks." The infant, whose brief life had ended the month Slim was born, had no history or identity, only a name fated to live again.

The new Erin left the county clerk's office with a stamped birth certificate to replace the one she'd told the clerk she'd lost.

The new hairstyle and look had been Gracie's inspiration. When Slim told her, on the steps of the municipal building, that she had a new name, Gracie said, "Well, you still look like my regular Mommy."

By the time Mustapha's truck came to pick them up, she didn't. The woman holding Gracie's hand as they climbed the rickety steps to their new shelter, had short auburn hair and was plainly outfitted, except for a single, strange accessory, a watch set in a clunky plastic bracelet.

"Yuck." Gracie had evaluated her mother's new appearance. "Yuck," she whispered again, when she saw their new home. Two small mattresses on the floor in a house crowded with temporarily homeless Arabs.

"I'm sorry," Mustapha said, without having heard Gracie's appraisal, "this is the best we can—"

Silencing her daughter with a look, Erin Shleeter cut him off. "It's fine. Thanks."

The tall, dark man shrugged apologetically and left them.

Gracie holding tight to her mother's hand, gaped at their roommates. "Mom," she whispered, "who are all those people?"

"They're kind of . . . they're friends of friends of Phil," Slim offered, tossing their newly purchased vinyl bags onto the floor next to their mattresses.

"Yeah, but . . . " Gracie stared at her mother. "They're *strangers.*"

The next days were a bureaucratic nightmare, and a success—with "Erin" applying for and getting a social security card, a driver's license, credit cards, and a job.

The job was working for Mustapha and Hassam at Double D Harbor Rentals. The only thing left was to find a safe school and get Gracie admitted to it.

In the meantime, Gracie played inside the rental office, mostly on the floor between Mustapha's desk and her mother's. Bored, she colored, threw crumpled paper "basketballs" into the wastebaskets and, each evening, ate the hearty, mysterious food shared by fifteen other people at the big table in Mustapha's kitchen.

"Arabs are like underground railroad," Mustapha said, one afternoon, handing her mother an Airborne Express package. "Phil says don't worry. He is not deported."

She opened the package addressed to Erin Shleeter. Inside was a second parcel, this one addressed to Slim c/o the Red Car Diner.

"Did Phil say anything to me?" Gracie asked, as Erin tore open the smaller envelope.

"Naturally!" Mustapha assured her. "He say, 'How is favorite girl?' I tell him, 'A beautiful lady now.'"

Gracie beamed. Slim gasped. "It's . . . from my father," she said. "You remember, Gracie, the man we met in that big loft in San Francisco?"

"Yuck." Gracie wrinkled her nose. "He wasn't nice."

"No, he wasn't," Slim said, stunned but unable to keep herself from grinning. "I guess he had a change of heart."

• • •

He'd been called irresponsible, immature, selfish, but no one had ever called Jupiter unadventurous. So when three obviously fake FBI men crashed his office, he'd responded graciously at first, sensing an escapade in the offing.

His visitors were indifferent to manners. "Let's cut the bullshit, fella," one of them said, unaware that Jupiter's craggy face had hardened. "We're looking for the woman who came to see you yesterday. She's wanted on charges of kidnapping."

"Really?" Jupiter said, coolly. "Can one 'kidnap' one's own child?" Picking up the ring that Slim had left with him, he turned it in his hand.

"I'm just here to tell you," a ponytailed wacko stressed, "that if you help the broad in any way, you're toast, you know what I mean?"

"Not really," Jupiter said. "Enlighten me."

"He means dead," the largest of the phony Feds translated. "If she shows up again, you better call this number." He threw a card onto Jupiter's desk, which the totally composed venture capitalist neither looked at nor lifted. Shortly after the trio left, Jupiter composed a short letter.

It was the note Erin was reading now.

"Yesterday three men threatened to kill me if I helped you in any way. Fortunately for you, this aroused my interest. I'm sending this to an old address, the diner where you worked. If this reaches you and you need more, leave word at my office—Jupiter."

She had already dug through the gift wrap and found: Cash. Fifties. Probably a couple thousand dollars. Still grinning, she fought the impulse to cry. But failed.

Mustapha and his friends—who had treated Gracie like a little queen or, at least, like the children she reminded them of, the ones they'd left behind and were hoping to send for some-day—helped carry the second-hand furniture Erin had bought into the small, pretty home Jupiter's money had provided.

Gracie pitched in, carrying little packages and shopping bags of food. But she wasn't happy about leaving Mustapha's house. Much as she'd longed for it, parting from fifteen doting brothers, fathers and friends was a big price to pay for a room of her own.

The small house wasn't anything like their old abode, but in Erin's eyes, it was perfect. All it needed was a security system. After hanging sheets as makeshift curtains over the windows, Erin grabbed a hammer and pounded a two by four over the back door. It had a thick rope attached to it. "Mommy, what's that for?" Gracie asked, watching in awe.

"To protect you and keep you safe, Toots," Erin answered. "So, what do you think?" she asked. "You like this place?"

"Why?" Gracie asked suspiciously, "are we moving again?"

"No. We just—"

"Good," Gracie announced. "Because, Mom, I am sick and tired to death of moving!"

"Me, too. So here's the deal." Slim made a peanut butter and jelly sandwich and handed it to her daughter. "While we're here, remember to call me Mom or Erin, but not Slim, okay?"

"I never call you Slim," Gracie said. "And how come I can't have that lamb stuff like at Mustapha's?"

Erin rolled her eyes. "I'll get the recipe," she said. "And I know you don't call me Slim, kiddo, but—"

"I don't think you are that Slim," Gracie grumbled.

"Thanks a lot."

"Do I get a new name too?" she asked, shuffling upstairs with Erin for her bath.

"I guess." Erin hadn't thought of that. It wasn't a bad idea. "If you want one."

"Okay," Gracie said. And while her mother was pulling from the bath bucket, rubber duckies, wind-up fish, and the sailboat Hassam had whittled for her, Gracie's eyes lit up. "Mom," she called excitedly. "I have a good idea."

– 125 –

• • •

"Are you sure?" Erin asked her daughter, a few days later, as they walked up the path to the pre-school she'd finally chosen.

"Better than Erin," Gracie said, defensively.

"Okay. Here goes." The pre-school director was waiting in front of the building. Erin extended her hand. "Excuse me, Betty? Hi, I'm Erin Shleeter. I called you—"

"Oh, hi," the Director said. "And who is this?"

"This is my daughter," Erin hedged.

"Look at you." Betty knelt to greet Gracie. "You're so cute. What's your name?"

"Queen Elizabeth," Gracie said, proudly.

Betty blinked and looked up at Erin for affirmation. Erin shrugged, smiled. That's my daughter, she seemed to say.

• • •

On Sundays, they went for their ride in the secondhand Taurus that Mustapha had found for them. This Sunday, Erin's driving seemed especially reckless, too fast, as if she wanted to get it over with.

"You know, Mom?" Queen E commented from her backseat perch, her lips white with powdered sugar. "I like the doughnuts and talk-ing to Grandma, but every Sunday, to drive for fifty-five hours—?"

"It's not fifty-five." Erin sounded exasperated. She'd grown to like Mitch's mother, even to depend on her, but there was no way around it, Mrs. Hiller was a link between their past and present; a weekly reminder that she and her regal daughter were living a double life and one that was tenuously safe at best.

"—Just to reach some phone booth?! Hey can I call Daddy this time? Please? Please, please, please. . . "

Erin shook her head. Queen E gave her a mournful look.

"Oh for pity's sake, don't beg," Erin said, "You look like a dog."

They stopped at a country store out in the sticks. The pay phone was on the porch. Erin dialed the number, Queen E at her side.

Mrs. Hiller answered right away. "He's plan-ning some legal action, now," she told her daughter-in-law. "You're depriving him of his rights as a father, some nonsense like that. But unfortunately, as you know, he has friends in the police department—"

"What are you saying?" Erin asked.

"Talk to him," Mitch's mother urged. "Please. You'd better call him right now, calm him down."

"Oh, swell."

"Dear." Mrs. Hiller didn't know what to call her. "It might help if he talked to Gracie. For her sake, too. I mean you of all people should know it's not healthy to be without a father."

Erin said she'd think about it. "We'd better keep this short. Talk to you next week, okay?" She hung up and started for the car, anxiously nibbling on her lower lip. As she went, she glanced behind her at Queen E, who, thanks to Assad's guidance, was bouncing a basketball with one hand behind her back. Erin's pace slowed. She stopped. Shaking her head, she walked back toward her daughter.

"Come on, your majesty," she said, "Let's call Daddy, okay?"

Queen Elizabeth cradled the receiver with two hands while Erin dialed. A moment later, the child's face lit up. "Hi Daddy!" she shouted. "We're having a great vacation!" After a listening pause, she went on. "Oh, we've been everywhere. Chicago . . . just the airport, though. And—"

Erin shook her head and took the receiver away. "No questions, okay?" she said into the phone, "or it ends now." Quickly, not wanting to even hear his voice, she handed the phone back to Queen E.

"Listen, bitch, she's my daughter too," Mitch shouted. "And I have a right to talk to her any goddamn way I want to."

Queen E listened. Even Erin could hear Mitch yelling. "Just tell him you love him and say goodbye, okay?" she told the stunned child.

Queen E nodded, frowning now. "Goodbye." Without saying I love you, she gave her mother the receiver. Erin hung up. "I am really, really sad," the child said.

Angry at herself, Erin knelt and hugged her daughter. "And I am really, really sorry, kiddo. My mistake."

• • •

In a characterless office, in a police station, hundreds of miles away, Mitch reached over and pressed OFF on his cell phone. It was sitting in a hands-free speaker-phone holder on a desk nicked with cigarette burns, carved initials and obscenities. "What do you think?" he asked the guy sitting on the other side of the desk. The man's handsome head was lowered, studying his tented fingers.

Behind him, cops, both uniformed and plain-clothes, were visible through the thick glass wall. "Robbie!" Mitch grumbled.

The rose-toting, poetry reader from the diner looked up. "Huh?"

"About her voice."

"What?" he asked, flashing his pearly whites at Mitch. "She sounds the same."

"Good. Yeah," Mitch said, "Because in case she's changed her appearance—"

"I remember her, man," Robbie assured him. "I told you before. From the diner, the scam. The only thing I don't remember is why you broke the rules and decided to marry the bitch."

Mitch bristled. "She's not a bitch."

Robbie rolled his cold blue eyes. "Oh, sorry. She's a waitress."

"What's that mean?" Mitch demanded.

"It means she's stupid! To call your mother? And now she's calling you?" The cop gestured lazily to the map on his office wall, a map of Northern Michigan. Pay Phones, a title on the map read. On it were pins, and next to each the date the calls were placed.

"She's not stupid," Mitch asserted. "She thinks what everybody thinks. That if you keep the call short it can't be traced."

"I still want to know, with all the girls we pulled that on, why her?" Robbie asked.

Mitch stood up, shrugged, irritated, "Maybe it's love, Robbie?"

With a dry chuckle, the cop said, "Yeah, right," made an obscene gesture, added, "I know what that means." Then advised, "If you were smart, you'd forget her."

Mitch leaned across the desk. "I can't forget her! She kidnapped my goddamn kid!"

Robbie got up and closed the door so other officers couldn't hear them. "How many times do I have to go there?" he asked Mitch, exasperated. "Kidnapping's when somebody who isn't the mother takes the kid. When the mother takes the kid, it's parenting, okay?"

Mitch wasn't up for a lecture. "How soon can you get there?"

"I don't know," Robbie groused. "Hey, I've got a job here. This whole idea—"

"You've got lots of jobs here," Mitch cut him off. "And the department doesn't know all the extra ways you make money, does it?"

Robbie glanced over his shoulder. The office door was closed, but that didn't mean Mitch's voice wouldn't carry over the partition. Two plainclothes guys passing his cubicle gave him crafty smiles. "Screw you," Robbie whispered to

Mitch. "You've got to be reasonable, huh? I know guys in Detroit who can handle—"

"Like your guys in Seattle? I know what they're like. They never met her, never heard her voice. She'll spot them and run before they even see her." Mitch stood up. He towered over the edgy cop. "It's you, Robbie," he said in a quiet voice that was twice as threatening as his shouted demands. "It's you, or . . . " Mitch smiled, grimly. "It's just you."

Robbie stared at him, trying to read his intentions. "Oh, shit. You're going to kill her, aren't you?"

"How can you say that, Rob?" Still grinning, Mitch sounded aggrieved. "You know how I am with women. You've seen me with Charlene and the extraordinary Rita . . . "

Robbie kept staring at him. And Mitch stared back. After a moment, the cop lowered his eyes, beaten. "Some day, man," Robbie said softly, "I want you to explain something. Why is it that I always do whatever the hell you want?"

● ● ●

"Well, you said you wanted it." Hands on her hips, Erin stood over Queen E, watching the child poke politely at the lumpy lamb stew on her plate. "I couldn't reach Assad at Mustapha's so I just, you know, winged it. What do you think, is it okay? It's okay, right?"

Queen E nodded without conviction.

"No, it's not. It's horrible," Erin acknowledged.

"It's not *horrible*, Mom." Her daughter was trying to be diplomatic.

"But it's not good, is it?" she pressed, knowing she should have left well enough alone. "Is it good?"

"Good?" Incredulous, Queen Elizabeth looked at her mother. "Mom, *you* tasted it."

Erin slid back into her seat, pushed her plate back, and hung her head. In a second, silent tears flooded down her face.

This was not what Queen E was up for. And, after gagging on lamb lumps and lying like Pinocchio, she wasn't about to try comforting her mother again. Better to just move on. "Know what I think?" she said, wisely.

Erin pulled herself together. "What's that?"

"I think you miss Daddy."

The diagnosis was so wrong, so wacky, that it was almost touching. Almost. Erin felt compelled to be honest. "Daddy yells at me, Toots."

Queen E nodded, sighed, thought. Finally, she said, "Well. You miss somebody."

Erin laughed, and hugged her daughter. And after her highness was asleep, she began to quietly gather up some of Gracie's clothing from the floor. Half visible under the bed, she found a flannel shirt. It was Joe's. The one Gracie had worn the night they'd fled Joe's house.

She looked at it. Smiled. Smelled it.

NOT ALL
MEN . . .

J oe got off the plane with his carry-on luggage and went directly to the bank of pay phones. Tossing back his disheveled dark hair, switching the arm his jacket was folded over, he examined the numbers on the phones, comparing them to the one he'd memorized. That one rang a few minutes later. He picked it up and said, "Sorry, my plane was delayed."

At Double D Harbor Rentals, Erin smiled. "Okay, rent a car, make sure you're not followed and drive to Green Bay. Go to Starbucks, not the three on Main Street or the one by the library. The one in the bookstore. There's a pay phone there."

Joe shook his head, and tried not to let her hear his laugh. "What is this, a treasure hunt? Am I going to spend the whole weekend flying around?"

He sounded so good, so eager and full of mischievous pleasure. "Don't worry, you'll be here by four, I promise," she said. "I'll call you at Starbucks in three hours." Then she hung up.

Dutifully, Joe dragged over to the rent-a-car counter. Two and a half hours later, he found the bookstore Starbucks, doused his face with cold water, ordered a double espresso, and waited near the phone, enduring the glare of the only teenager in Green Bay without a cell phone.

• • •

At five minutes to four, Joe carried his luggage along the narrow aisle of cars to the front of the ferry's car deck.

He passed right by Robbie's Yukon where, a map of Michigan spread out on the seat beside him with several towns circled and crossed out, Mitch's cop was asleep at the wheel.

On the dock, redheaded Erin and her royal daughter were waiting. They saw Joe before he saw them. Their excited shouts were drowned out by the ferry's crackling loudspeaker calling, "Attention passengers. Prepare for arrival."

The announcement woke Robbie. He stretched and took a sip of cold coffee from his Starbucks cup. Suddenly a distant voice cut through all the other sounds: "Hey, Joe! Hey! Over here!"

Robbie blinked, cocked his head. Had he just heard what he thought he heard? The waitress. Hiller's runaway wife.

Joe heard her, too. And waved as Queen E jumped up and down on the dock shouting, "Joe! Joe! Joe!"

Robbie leaped out of his car and stood on the sideboard for a decent view. He saw the wife, pitifully disguised as some redheaded housefrau. And the kid. And, waving back, just up ahead, the guy he'd sent his crew to hassle, Slim's old school buddy, Joe.

The ferrymen dropped the bridge and foot passengers started to walk off. The waitress and Mitch's kid were still jumping up and down. Robbie watched them join up with Joe College. Watched them hugging the sap.

Then he saw that there were three cars ahead

of his in his lane. He watched nervously as Mitch's family led the guy toward their car. The walk-ons were off the boat. The first cars started to unload. In a couple of seconds, Robbie would be driving off, too.

"Most preposterous trip I ever made in my life," Joe was saying as Erin tossed his bags into the backseat. "I can tell you this much," he added, laughing. "I guarantee I was not followed."

"Joe, Joe, wait," Queen E called suddenly, taking his hand and pulling him away from the car. "You want to see where my Mommy works? If you stand on your tiptoes and look all the way over there, by the harbor, where that big D is, that's the place!"

Behind the wheel, Robbie tapped his foot impatiently. Finally, the car in front of his disembarked. He started to drive forward, trying to keep an eye peeled for the big reunion, when the ferry guy stepped in front of him and banged on the hood of his Yukon, signaling him to stop—then waving for the outside lane to go instead.

Outraged, Robbie peered ahead, and saw his target trio getting into Erin's car. He honked his horn, which irritated the ferry guy who shot him a no-deal, buddy look, and blithely signaled more cars from the next lane to move forward.

A minute later he watched in horror as Mitch's wife drove away, while he was stuck on the ferry to Bum Fuck. Robbie had an urge to beat in the old guy's brain, then flash his police I.D. as a finale. But that was all he needed. To have calls flying back and forth between the local cops and his precinct house where, if he failed Mitch Hiller, he'd wind up hawking his badge on E-bay.

• • •

Joe followed the two girls down the hall of their new home. "And this is the guest bedroom," redheaded Erin said, showing him Queen E's room, "normally known as Buckingham Palace."

Clearly Queen E had decorated her quarters herself. The walls, a hodgepodge of vivid smears and muddied paint drips, were, Joe had to admit, "Very . . . er, colorful."

"I made it," the child pointed out proudly.

"You'd better warn him," Erin prompted her daughter. When Queen E looked confused, Erin whispered in her ear. "Oh, yeah," the pleased little girl said. "The dreams in here get really noisy."

Joe set down his suitcase. "Really. What kind of noises, Gracie?"

She frowned. "My name is Queen Elizabeth."

"Right. Sorry, your highness," Joe quickly amended.

"No problem," Queen E said, regally. "Mom, what should we do tomorrow?"

Erin looked at Joe. "What would you like to do?"

"Just, you know, be together," Queen E answered.

"My thoughts exactly," Joe agreed.

Erin had to work for a while in the morning, so Joe and Queen E hung out near the harbor rental office waiting for her. With Joe holding her hand, the five-year-old daredevil walked around the railing of a boat in dock for repairs.

An odd sound, like a camera shutter snapping, made them both look up. As they stared at the repair yard, the noise repeated. Joe picked Queen E up and looked over at the dock with its warehoused boats and workers in safety glasses using sanding and welding tools. Any one of the odd-looking mechanical devices in the yard seemed capable of clicking or clacking. Still, Joe realized, the noise had raised goose bumps on his arms.

His eyes did a slow 180 around the area, and

stopped at the sight of Erin standing in the door-way of Double D, watching them. A gentle smile lit her face. She stepped out, squinting in the sunlight, and waving to them. "Okay. I'm ready," she called. And Joe heard the noise again.

They picnicked near the water and watched as Queen E showed off her new moves, bouncing her basketball wildly around the boardwalk.

"She seems to be doing great," Joe said.

"She is," Erin agreed.

"How about you? Are you okay? Cut off from everything. You can't talk to your friends or—"

Erin stopped him. **Putting** a finger to his lips, she explained **the situation** in two words: "Gracie's safe."

As the words left Erin's mouth, the basketball careened off Queen E's foot and rolled down the boardwalk.

"Yeah?" Joe said, "but Mitch is . . . when is this custody thing?"

"Not for a couple of months—"

"Anyway, they favor the mother, so—"

"Usually they do. But he has lots of money and lots of lawyers."

"That's kind of what I mean," Joe said. He considered asking her about the clacking sound. Had she heard it, just then? Was it a cam-

- 141 -

era of some kind? Or a tool they used in the boatyard? But he decided against it. They had so little time together and she'd been through enough. There was no reason to spook her because he didn't know squat about what went on around a harbor. "You look great," he said.

"Yeah." She laughed. "Constant fear is my beauty secret."

• • •

The basketball rolled until it hit someone's feet—a guy in dark glasses and a baseball cap, with a digital camera stuffed into the pocket of his team jacket. Queen E approached him, stopped.

"Hey there, Gracie, is this your ball?" the man said.

"Yup," the child replied, not noticing that he'd used her name, her old name.

"I'm Robbie," he said. "You want to learn a trick?"

• • •

"Slim," Joe was saying, "you can't run forever."

"Erin," she reminded him. "And why not? I'm good at it."

"You sure are. Then again, you're good at everything."

She eyed him suspiciously. "You criticizing me or flirting with me? Pick one."

"Both, I think."

Out of nowhere, out of pure instinct, Erin asked suddenly, "Where's Gracie?" She looked around.

Joe looked, too. "I don't know, she was just here . . . "

Erin squinted, frowning. There was no sign of her daughter. She felt panic rising in her chest, creeping into her throat. It wasn't like her to just disappear.

Joe sprinted down the boardwalk. "Elizabeth!"

"Elizabeth?" Erin called, not sure which name to shout.

Could it be that Mitch had found them again? *No.* Erin wouldn't even allow the thought to enter her mind. "Elizabeth— Gracie—where are you?"

Jumping frantically to her feet, she started to call out again, when, from a completely different direction than the one she was facing, Queen Elizabeth hollered, "Hey, Mom. You want to see this?"

Erin jumped.

She was right there, perfectly fine, holding her basketball.

"Sure," Erin said, trying to calm herself down. See? It was nothing. She'd been there all along.

Queen E concentrated fiercely and started to dribble the ball.

Erin wasn't paying attention. Shivering, she couldn't shake the odd and awful sensation that her child was in danger. She continued to look around warily. And as she looked, the man in the baseball cap, his head down, the collar of his jacket pulled up, walked right past her.

• • •

It took a long time for the feeling to pass. It lingered into the night.

Even after the three of them were settled peacefully in their rooms, Slim couldn't rest. With Gracie snuggled comfortably beside her, looking angelic in the soft light of the bedside lamp, Slim kept a weary vigil.

She must have fallen asleep for a little while, though, because her eyes flew open at the sound of someone rummaging in the kitchen.

It was Joe. With a glass of juice in his hand, he

peered into her bedroom on the way back to his.

"Hey," she greeted him.

"Gracie was right," he said in a half-whisper. "About the dreams in there."

"Yeah, mine are pretty loud, too," she confessed. After a moment, she tossed her head, inviting him in. "You remember the house rules?" she said, as he got into bed.

He held her hand in both of his, rubbing it gently because it was cold. "With Gracie here? Who can forget?"

"Joe?" she said, after a while, lulled by his warmth and tenderness.

"Yeah."

"What would've happened . . . if, you know, if you and I—"

"Don't," he whispered. "It's stupid to think like that."

"Why?" she asked.

He had to think about it for a moment. "Well, for one thing," he answered, "because of Gracie. She's awesome, Slim. Gracie is truly a great kid. And any path that doesn't include her doesn't make sense."

She squeezed his hand, nodded. "Ginny told me about that weekend."

"Ginny? Right. The weekend of your wedding?"

"Yes."

"She tell you how terrible I was?"

"Joe." Slim smiled and shook her head. "That might work on other people, but you forget. I've actually *had* you."

"Trust me. I didn't forget."

"And I'm telling you, from memory," she added dreamily, "you're not that bad."

For a second he wasn't sure. Then they both laughed.

"Do you really have to go tomorrow?" she asked, affectionately.

Joe nodded.

"Couldn't you quit your job, and stay here, and play the horses or something, become independently wealthy?"

He didn't say anything, just held her hand. Finally, he turned toward her, quietly serious. "Please kiss me, Slim," he said, "I know we're not supposed to, it's against house rules, but for me to come all this way and feel the way I do and for us to not even—"

She kissed him. Every part of her body responded to the warm urgency of his lips. For a moment, the fear drained out of her, replaced by a startling rush of exhilaration and comfort, yearning and safety . . .

There was a movement outside the window. A

shadow that might have been a tree swaying. A sound like a branch tapping once against the glass. A twig breaking, an animal scurrying, a strange muffled click.

Shivering, she pulled away from Joe. Nothing was really safe as long as she and Gracie were being hunted. Not even—or maybe, especially— love.

BUT YOU CAN'T HIDE

During the day, she is Erin again. Homemaker Erin with her eccentric, inventive daughter, stirring up a batter of banana chocolate chip pancakes for supper.

Good Mommy Erin, bundling her chatty child in after-bath towels, combing out the tangles in her squeaky clean hair, watching a pale rainbow of fingerpaint swirl down the drain.

Read-to-Me Erin, sitting at the edge of the bed, chanting Dr. Seuss rhymes, until the beau-

tiful dark lashes of her regal baby flutter to still-
ness and sleep.

As night falls on the secluded house, Erin
breathes a sigh of contentment, for another day
of "normal life" has passed. And it is only at
night, just before she sinks into slumber, that
she can allow herself the knowledge that she is
really Slim.

Outside, the streetlamps have dulled, and
even the moon is shrouded by clouds. Inside,
everything is dark and quiet, except for the
occasional moans of an old house—a floor-
board creaks, a clock ticks, the walls settle. . .

Gracie's room is dim in the shadows of her
nightlight. She is huddled under her covers,
teddy bear clutched in her hands, her breathing
hushed and even.

Slim's bedroom door is open. She lies flat in
her bed, listening, concentrating on tomorrow's
plans, worrying about Gracie. . . and yawning.

Stop thinking. Get to sleep, she tells herself, and
flutters her eyelids, briefly glimpsing the hall. . .

A face flashes in the hallway mirror.

She sits up, shivering.

A familiar pair of dark eyes is meeting her
gaze, pinning her down with a calm, cold,
unforgiving stare.

God, no. It can't be.

Mitch!

She tries to scream, but her voice is strangled. . . .

●　●　●

GASP.

Slim awoke with a start, heart pounding like a jackhammer. The first light of dawn grayed her window. She sat up suddenly, hands outstretched and trembling, and looked around. Everything was normal. Peaceful. Safe.

Her nostrils flared slightly, catching a pale scent that reminded her of a bar—aftershave, sweet and stinging, mixed with cigarette smoke and stale beer. She rubbed her nose, and shook her head, trying to clear away the frightening dream. *All just a nightmare*, she reminded herself, to calm her labored breathing. Instinctively she touched her wrist, fingered the special plastic bracelet she'd bought that first week of being Erin.

The air crept into her skin. Her bedroom was cold, so frigid that all she wanted to do was nestle into the sheets, and rest, and forget—but she couldn't. She had to pee. Damn.

Slim gritted her teeth, tossed aside the covers, padded to the window. There was glistening frost on the ground, on the trees. And dark muddy tire marks where, for some reason, the frost hadn't settled . . .

She moved down the hall. Her nightmare trailed her. Every open door felt like a trap ready to spring; each shadow seemed new, human and tall. She glanced into Queen Elizabeth's room, barely able to curb the insane fear that her daughter would be gone. But no, the exhausted little Queen was still curled up in her bed, sleeping calmly.

Relieved, Slim wandered next into the bathroom. She pulled down her pajamas to pee. The chill of the tile floor pricked her feet, waking her, alerting her senses. In the early morning daylight, everything seemed sharper: the colors of the bathroom tile, the smell of her pungent soap, the tiny sounds of her house creaking.

The shower curtain in front of her, rustling.

She stared at the curtain while sitting on the toilet, watched it stir. *Just the wind,* she decided, but could not help the steady thread of panic running up her spine: *Something is wrong.*

The curtain rustled again.

Thoughts immediately sprang to her mind. *Gracie? But Gracie was in her bedroom, asleep . . . they* were *alone, weren't they?*

Heart thudding, she wiped herself, pulled up her pants, and took a deep breath.

One. Two. Three.

In one swift move, Slim yanked back the curtain—

Nothing.

It was nothing: just a quiet and empty white stall, just the breeze sweeping through the old house's warped window frames. *I'm really going crazy,* she thought.

Combing her fingers through her hair, she hurried down the hall and into the kitchen, filled the kettle with water and set it on the stove. She drank a little O.J. from a carton at the fridge, then entered the living room, pausing to fold a sweater. She was still trembling. The house still didn't feel right.

And this time, as she looked up, her worst intuitions were confirmed.

A tall man leaped into her path—grabbing her—real, hard, fast. He stood above her, smirking.

It was Mitch.

MITCH!

She faltered in disbelief, gasping heavily. She wanted to shriek, but, somehow, remembering her sleeping daughter, managed to stifle the noise. *Okay*, Slim tried to convince herself, *everything's going to be okay*, though a terrible fear washed over her body. *How had he found her this time?*

Mitch wrenched her arm, pulling her along the corridor, slamming her against one wall, then the other. Slim fought him, her jaws locked against the fierce cry welling up inside her. He was far too strong, stronger than she remembered. She had no chance. Still, she resisted, scratched, clawed, tried to kick, tried to knee him.

The only sounds were grunts, their bodies heaving into walls and her head, clamped in his hands, being banged against the doorframe to her room. He spun her into a vicious headlock and, putting his mouth close to her ear, whispered intensely.

"I want you back," he hissed.

"No," she said.

"Everything will be just like it was."

She jerked in his grasp, trying to loosen his grip on her. "I told you!" she spat through clenched teeth, "No!" Even she was startled by the speed and forcefulness of her response when her life was, literally, in his hands.

"That's pretty stupid," he warned. "You know

why?" His hands moved to her neck. And squeezed. "Because if I can't have you, nobody will."

She clawed against his hands, trying to pry them loose.

"Like that jerk," Mitch said, "who was here with you? He'll be fishing for his guts in Lake Washington."

The pressure on her Adam's apple was beyond painful. Gagging, aching, every breath she tried to draw sent shockwaves to her brain. Odd shapes and colors flashed inside her eyelids. She was close to blacking out.

"Know what else, hon?" Mitch was saying, as he bent over her, "For murder, they need a body. Otherwise, they'll think you disappeared again."

Determined to stay conscious, Slim opened her eyes, pulled on his hands with all her might. As she did, she saw past him. She saw Queen E standing in the doorway of her painted room. Watching.

"Only this time, you won't ever come back," Mitch rasped, breathlessly.

"No!" Queen E shouted suddenly. "No! Mommy! Stop it! Stop it! Stop it!" As she screamed, she ran to them and began beating her fists on her father's back, pulling his hair.

He seemed not to hear her, not to feel her. He didn't stop, didn't even hesitate. Despite his daughter's screams, he kept strangling Slim. Ignoring Gracie, he whirled and slammed against the child, throwing her back against the wall.

Slim heard it, saw it in a blur. Beyond desperate, she stopped clawing at Mitch's hands and grabbed her own, fingers straining toward the thick plastic bracelet around her wrist, reaching for the watch face while her daughter shrieked and sobbed.

Getting no air now, Slim turned the front of the bangle on her wrist so it pointed toward Mitch's face. At the last instant, he realized what it was and started to pull away. It was too late, then. She pressed the button. The pepper spray hit his face, his eyes. He roared in pain, releasing her at last.

Slim leaped up, grabbed Queen E and ran as Mitch writhed on the floor. She burst out the back door. Whirling, she pulled a rope, the thick rope she had installed. A two by four attached to it slid abruptly, blocking the door, locking it.

She sprinted for her Taurus, still in her pajamas, still carrying her child. She punched the code into the number pad on the driver's door, tore open the door, put Queen E inside and pulled the key from under the mat. Firing up the car, she hit the gas and rocketed away.

She should have ached, felt tired, her mind dulled from lack of oxygen. Instead, her senses, greased with adrenaline, were hyper sharp. From down the block, so far back she should not have heard it, a neighbor's car revved up. Slim checked the rearview mirror and saw a black Chevy Suburban pulling out of a driveway.

Hitting the highway, then winding through a maze of city streets, she pulled into a deserted strip mall. Parking in back, near the dumpsters, Slim jumped out of the Taurus, ran around to the trunk, and took out a small suitcase.

Moments later, she and Queen E were inside the car, pulling clothing from the suitcase, getting dressed.

"Mom, what's happening?" her daughter's lip was quivering.

"Just put this on, Gracie. Now! Hurry!" She threw a jacket into the back seat.

Distracted, in a frantic blur of pajamas and underwear and jeans, it took her an instant to hear the knock at the window and see the man staring in at them.

Time stopped, receded, as she stared at his

face. She was back at the diner. Years ago. He was the jerk with the rose, the guy Mitch had trashed.

What was he doing here, now?

In a flash, she knew. He was with Mitch. He had always been with Mitch. The fight they'd had at the Red Car had been a setup. Which meant that Mitch had lied to her from the beginning. He'd been phony from the moment she met him.

The man, Robbie, reached for her door handle. Slim slammed down the lock, and rammed the accelerator, leaving him behind. Her car shot forward, heading for the dumpsters. Desperately, she spun the wheel, swerving, kissing off the huge metal bin.

Mitch's pal was running for his car, the Chevy Suburban she'd seen down her block. It was hidden behind some nearby bushes. Which gave her time to pogo over a concrete divider and spin out onto the road.

As Robbie jumped into his Suburban, Slim, half in, half out of her clothing, was driving while trying to see her daughter, who was in her car seat but had not pulled down the locking bar.

"Car seat! Car seat! Pull down your—"

Gracie was trying to. "Then slow down," she hollered, "so I—"

"I can't slow down!" her mother shouted.

"Who was that guy?!" Gracie wanted to know.

Slim checked the rearview. "I don't know, some—" He was chasing them. "Oh, damn!" she grumbled, gunning the car even faster.

He stayed on their tail, chasing them, forcing them to accelerate through potholes, narrow alleyways, stop signs and red lights. Freaked out to be driving so fast and recklessly, Slim clutched the wheel and kept trying to tell Gracie, who was screaming wildly in the backseat, to hold on, hang in, that they were going to be all right.

"Hold on, honey," Slim gritted her teeth. "Mommy has a plan." She had hoped to never have to use it, but was glad she'd prepared for the worst.

Meanwhile, Gracie was trying to be brave, but Slim knew it was impossible. Gracie was four going on five and had just witnessed her father choking her mother, had been thrown across the floor by him, then snatched up by her terrified mother. And now she was in the back of a wildly speeding car trying to escape from a maniac out to kill them. So she screamed. She screamed clear out of the city and back onto rutted, winding country roads.

Mitch's buddy's Suburban was close behind them and getting closer, until, finally, it slammed into the Taurus, knocking it half off the road. Shouting for them to stop, to pull over, Robbie pushed them off again and again. Gracie covered her eyes, cried, screamed. Slim, coming back onto the pocked dirt trail, fought to keep control as the road narrowed down to one tight lane.

Peeking through her fingers, Gracie yelped, "Mom! Stop it!"

Up ahead, at a construction site, a steel bridge whose girders were being repaired crossed over a deep chasm. A thick metal bar had been placed across the bridge's access; low enough to keep trucks out but, Slim was betting, just tall enough for her Taurus to squeak under. "Mommy, no!" Gracie hollered, as Slim floored the accelerator aiming for the bridge.

A quick glimpse in the mirror, showed her Robbie's face, driven, confident, and full of blood lust. Then his expression changed. His eyes widened as he realized, too late, that the steel bar closing the bridge was too low for his SUV to pass beneath—

The Taurus rammed through, the bar scraping the roof, sending up a screeching hail of sparks.

The Suburban took the bar mid-windshield,

shattering the glass and collapsing the steel frame into a frowning brow. Gracie looked back at the smashed SUV, then looked at her mother. "Mom," she declared breathlessly, "that was dangerous."

Robbie crawled out, bloodied and furious. The last glimpse of him Slim caught in the rearview, he was banging his fists on the roof of the wreck and cursing up a storm.

• • •

With Mitch's pal out of the way she could have slowed down, but she didn't. She sped out into the country, keeping up a one-way conversation with Gracie. Although the child had stopped screaming, she was now staring straight ahead, looking terribly tired.

"Baby, just one more stop, okay? Then we won't have to drive so fast. Just hang in for a little while, Toots. And trust me. Are you okay, Gracie? That was scary, wasn't it? But it's going to be fine in a minute. One more minute. . . "

Slim pulled onto a dirt road and hit the brakes behind a rural barn. She jumped out of the Taurus and ran toward a white '78 Oldsmobile, parked under a rustic carport. Fishing for and finding keys under the car, she opened the trunk of the Olds and threw "Erin's" small suitcase on top of two larger bags inside. She ran around to the front and, reaching under the driver's seat, pulled out a wallet, checked its contents, and smiled gratefully, taking a deep breath at last.

Fifteen minutes later, driving along an empty two-lane highway, Slim pulled a red wig out of the glove compartment. She put it on as best she could, using one hand to tuck in the strands of her short auburn hair. "Okay, Toots," she said to Gracie, who was now belted into the backseat of the Olds, "we can talk."

Queen E stared at her. The ready giggle, the spark of mischief always in her eyes, even the temper that flared occasionally, were gone.

"Do you want me to tell you what happened?" Slim asked.

Her daughter blinked, then shook her head.

"Fair enough. One thing, though," she said, gently. "Erin is over."

Without expression, the child said, "I liked Erin."

Slim nodded sadly. She'd liked Erin, too. "You're not the Queen of England anymore either."

Gracie nodded and stared out the window. "I'm hungry," she said softly.

• • •

They'd driven south. The town they found themselves in was sunny and friendly and small. There was a well-tended square at the center of its business district. As she parked across the street from it, Slim noticed the impressive bronze plaque of Toller, Doyle, and Wexler, Attorneys at Law. On the opposite side of the square, there was a homey little café.

In her redheaded wig, Slim pushed food around her plate, trying to figure out their next move. Gracie ate voraciously. The battle with Mitch had taken its toll on both of them today. Slim's entire body ached. Her neck was tender and imprinted with red blotches where Mitch's fingers had dug in. Her throat ached. And she'd taken some hard falls.

Noticing Slim not eating, their waitress came over carrying her refill pot of coffee. "Everything okay here?" she asked, kindly.

Slim nodded. "Yes. Fine."

"Hey there, cutie," the woman said to Gracie, "I'm Milly. What's your name?"

Gracie glanced at her mother, then shrugged. "I don't know," she answered.

"She's working on it," Slim told the flustered woman.

After the waitress left them, Gracie said, in her new, expressionless voice, "Maybe I could be something regular this time. Like maybe Mary or Hassam." When Slim didn't respond, Gracie said, "Mom?"

"I'm thinking," Slim answered, distracted.

"Yeah," Gracie said, "I can hear it."

• • •

They climbed the stairs of the handsome brick building across the square to the lawyer's office. Slim sat Gracie down on a black leather sofa in the reception area, whispering to her, "You'll be okay?"

Gracie nodded dully, and looked down at her lap. Slim reached out to stroke her daughter's head, but Gracie ducked. "Be right back," she promised, studying the forlorn child for a moment. While it made Slim's heart ache, it also gave her courage. She went to the receptionist's desk and said, "Hi. Is Mr. Toller with someone?"

"No, but he's—" the tastefully dressed blonde began.

"I'm not a crazy person," Slim blurted, by way of explaining her next action, which was to walk swiftly past the receptionist and open the door behind her labeled James Toller, ESQ.

The blonde jumped up, as did a larger, more formidable woman at a second desk. But Slim was already inside, confronting the surprised but confident attorney. Jim Toller was in his early sixties, wearing an expensive white shirt, stylishly rumpled by blue suspenders. A tidy, distinguished white beard and closely-cropped white hair set off his kindly brown face, which was, at the moment, frowning at her.

"I don't know where you learned manners, young lady," he said with a hint of a genteel Southern accent, but this is not the way to get my attention."

"I know." Slim flashed a quick worried smile. "But I'm desperate." She looked around quickly, seeing the women watching her from the door, waiting for Toller's signal to get her out of there. "I got your name from a waitress, Millie something. You helped her husband with . . . I don't know, some suit from an ex-business partner."

She dug into her purse. "My husband keeps trying to kill me, and I need to talk to somebody

who's smart, Okay? Smarter than me, at least."
Pulling a sloppy handful of cash from her bag,
she pushed it across the desk at him. "This is all
the money I have. Well, all but twenty—It's
almost five hundred, and I'll give you all of it, if
you'll just listen to what ... happened ... just
two minutes, okay? Please?"

She was so intense and discombobulated, he
couldn't help but be intrigued. Against his better judgment, Toller signaled for his assistants
to leave. They backed out, cautiously leaving the
door slightly ajar.

"Um, the little person," Slim reminded
them, not wanting Gracie to hear the conversation.

The blonde nodded and shut the door.

Jim Toller did what she'd asked. He listened.
Tenting his fingers, leaning forward in his chair,
he took in every word. His poker face remained
impassive throughout her tale. And when she
was finished, he stared at the wad of bills she'd
set on his desk, and leaned back.

"Pardon my French, dear," he said in a soft,
not unkind voice, "but I hope you got some
pleasure from it, because you have really
screwed yourself."

Slim closed her eyes, feeling terror and tears
starting up.

"My dear, you had two chances to file a complaint." Toller stood and paced, keeping his eyes on her. "Two chances to go to the police and put his violence on record. You ignored both. Which tells him to keep coming until he kills you."

Startled, she looked up.

"As for your child, Gracie—" He perched at the edge of his desk. "You are planning to go to this custody hearing?"

"Yes, sir," Slim said.

"Good." Toller nodded. "If you didn't, the judge would rule against you and you'd become a fugitive. Once you're there, though, your husband will, as you say, portray you as a drug addict."

He let it sink in, then added, "For all I know, you are one. You break in here uninvited. I'd say your attacker has a very good chance to get sole custody. Now if you don't mind. . . " Pushing her money back at her, the lawyer got back into his chair and back to work.

Slim was stunned. "That's it? You're not going to help me?"

"That's what I'm telling you. It's too late. There isn't anyone who *can* help you."

She stared at him. His words seemed even more deadly and final coming from a complete stranger. Slim realized she should get up, leave, but she couldn't move.

Toller watched her. He had a thought. After evaluating whether he should or shouldn't share it, he said: "In good conscience, I should say the custody hearing is probably a trick."

Slim waited for him to say more. Carefully, he plucked a twenty-dollar bill from the stack she hadn't picked up yet. He showed it to her, wanting her to realize he was about to give her valuable advice. Advice she was paying for.

"The custody hearing? It's not about itself. It's a way to find you. To get you to a particular place at a particular time, so his men can follow you." He looked at her without flinching. "And he can come to wherever you are . . . and kill you."

She blinked. *Oh my God,* she thought. Of course. He was right.

• • •

Slim spent much of the day wandering the little town, with a silent, changed Gracie at her side, a Gracie who wasn't interested in a new drawing pad or coloring book or the Asian puppets in the window of the local toy store or rich chocolate pastries designed to look like mice.

It wasn't too late, Slim kept telling herself. Mr. Toller knew the law, but he didn't know her. There had to be something she could do. She could handle despair but not defeat. Not when the price of losing was Gracie.

She wasn't the smartest person she'd ever met. Or the gutsiest. And she wasn't strong, not physically anyway. Not compared to Mitch, who had her by a hundred pounds and nearly a foot in height. But being on her own, setting up the new house, carrying furniture and groceries and Gracie had given her a few new muscles and a lot of resourcefulness.

Toller had been weighing her legal options. But who said that saving her life and protecting her child was strictly a legal matter?

Earlier today, Gracie hadn't wanted to hear Slim's explanation of what was happening. But Slim had some things she wanted to tell her daughter. So, that night, for the first time, she allowed her to curl up in the front passenger seat, and decided to say what she had to say, whether Gracie heard it or not.

It was late. There were only a few cars on the road. Gracie was already asleep beside her by the time Slim thought it all through. Part of what she'd figured out meant that she and Gracie would be separated for a little while. At least, Slim hoped it would be only a little while. If she messed up—which she couldn't;

wouldn't, she told herself—the downside to her plan was that this might be the last night they'd ever spend together.

Slim glanced down at her daughter, then back at the road. As she drove, her hand caressed the sleeping child's cheek. "I've got to make you a promise, Grace," she began, softly, "Ever since you were born . . . well, one day, I started to think of all the awful things that were going to happen. Yeah, I know, I know," Slim said, as if Gracie were listening, "Pretty crazy, huh? But I did. I thought of . . . people you'd love who'd die . . . or leave you, betray you, break your heart . . . "

Gracie stirred. With one hand, Slim adjusted the sweatshirt covering the child, pulling it up over Gracie's shoulders and tucking it around her bare feet. "I thought of physical injuries," she continued. "Broken bones or sickness or guys who'd hurt you some way. And I thought that if I could protect you, even once, from any of those things . . . if I could absorb any part of that myself . . . "

Slim sighed. It wasn't going to be easy. "Well, Gracie," she said, "Here goes."

PART THREE

BATTLE

OF THE

SEXES

SAYING

GOODBYE

Hold hands, it's crowded," Ginny hollered at her children, as she made her way through the busy airport looking for the bank of phones Slim had specified. As she approached it, one of the phones started to ring. "Stop arguing," she warned her son and daughter, "You're going to break it." Irritably, she picked up the receiver. "This is the most ridiculous thing I've ever done," she grumbled.

"Oh, yeah? How about Horace?" Slim's voice asked.

Ginny glanced down at her kids who were fighting over a green, plastic action figure the way Horace, her ex, would've fought for beer. "Okay," she conceded, smiling against her will, "this is the *second* most."

Slim laughed, then reined it in and said, "Gin, rent a car, drive to Reno, then fly to San Jose."

Ginny's mouth fell open. "You're out of your mind."

"You noticed." Slim chuckled, then hung up.

Ginny stared at the receiver, shook her head in disbelief, and hung up, too. Herding her kids, she trudged toward the airport rental car counter. A few minutes later, they were in the parking garage, loading their bags into the back of a gleaming compact. As Ginny wheeled the luggage cart back to its rack, Slim popped out from behind a concrete pillar.

Ginny gasped, recognized her, hugged her. "Oh my God. What're you doing here? Look at you." She eyed Slim's short haircut. "I thought we were driving to Reno."

"I had to make sure you weren't followed," Slim explained, "God, it's good to see you."

Ginny checked out her hair, again. "I like it,"

she said, "Sort of." Then she noticed Gracie standing very quietly beside Slim. She knelt and held out her arms. "Hey, Graceland!"

At first, Gracie just blinked at her. Then, she gave Ginny a tepid hug. "Go on. The kids are in the back. They can't wait to see you," Ginny said. Obediently, Gracie walked over to the rental car. Ginny looked up at Slim.

"It's been very hard on her," Slim said, looking as though she might cry. "But it'll be over soon. At least, I know she'll be safe and have fun with you."

"Definitely. Me and my kids," Ginny cracked, "We're a barrel of laughs."

"Here." Slim held out a wallet. "Credit card, cash, plane tickets. It's on me, but make no calls home, or to Phil, okay? Think of it, you're finally taking those two months of paid vacation." She turned to Gracie who had started to climb into the car. "Toots?"

Gracie looked at her, then again tried to climb in, but Slim pulled her back into a hug. She held her for as long as Gracie would tolerate, then watched as her daughter scrambled into the backseat with Ginny's kids.

"I love you, Toots," Slim mouthed to her behind the window glass. Tears sprang to Slim's eyes.

"Take care of her, huh?" she said softly, turning to Ginny, "and if you need to reach me—" She handed Ginny a cell phone. "Just don't call anyone you know."

"Don't worry. Jimmy's going to teach her to dribble behind her back, by the time you see her—"

"Yeah. Thanks," Slim said. "If you need to reach me, I'm number one on the auto-dialer. Or I'll call you. Any calls between us have to run fifteen seconds or less. Cake?"

"Pie," Ginny said.

"Enjoy it, huh?"

"Slim," her friend called as she started to walk away, "How long?"

"The custody hearing is the end of next month. That's my deadline."

"Deadline for what?" Ginny asked.

Slim just looked at her.

"Everything."

THE
KNOWLEDGE

S lim moved from side to side in a controlled rhythm. Her speed was astonish-
ing; her eyes were as still and glazed as
Gracie's had been.

"I said, are you ready?" A deep, resonant male
voice echoed through the gym.

"Yeah," Slim said, stretching her neck, her
arms.

They circled, lunging, each trying to pull the
other off balance. The man was far taller than

Mitch, heavier, too, and all muscle. He'd been training for decades. Slim had been working with him for three and a half weeks.

"I want someone really good," she'd told Jupiter.

"How about better than that?" her father suggested, "How about the best?"

This man was it.

A gentle giant, Slim thought at first.

"A killer," Jupiter had said. "But legit. He did it for Uncle Sam."

If it were possible for someone to be both, her instructor, with his glistening coal black skin and softly commanding voice was the man.

Slim punched, her arm shooting out and back, out and back. There was no thought involved now. The minute she started a move, her body kicked in, took over. There was no question of how hard, how bad. Every move was thorough, final, full out.

"You sure?" he asked.

She'd been hitting him for weeks. One time with a fist; next time with an open palm, third time with a hammer punch. Repeating the sequence over and over. Her hands didn't hurt anymore. Her arms and shoulders no longer ached. She connected often now. And not because he was letting her.

"Uh-huh," Slim answered, still concentrating, breathing regularly, staring straight ahead.

For hours, she'd shot a hand out, fingers extended, into halved grapefruits. Wherever he held the half, however fast he moved it, she could puncture it—using two fingers or two thumbs. She could deflect or dodge a medicine ball. Slip under his punches.

At first, when he hit her with his padded mitts, she'd hyperventilate, duck, lose her balance, slide and fall. This week, finally, he'd swarmed all over her, hitting her, kneeing her, keeping her trapped, spinning her from side to side, trying to make her lose her cool.

The instant he let up, she punched back, hitting the mitts.

"Can you lose?" His question reverberated through the gym.

"No," she said.

"Can he hurt you?"

The first time he'd asked that, Slim had thought of Gracie, of what it would be like to live without her, for Mitch to have her and to lose it, his temper, his cool, whatever fragile rubberband held him together. What would happen if it snapped and Gracie was in the way?

But in the weeks she'd been studying with this man, working with this master, those possibilities had died along with the woman who would allow someone to beat her.

"No," she answered now.

"Even though he's bigger?"

"He's a lot bigger."

He had circled her, pushing her with a leather pad, the signal for her to attack. And she did. Punch after punch after punch into the pad he was holding.

"Even though he's stronger?" her instructor crooned.

"He's a lot stronger," Slim said.

He'd gone for her throat, almost exactly as Mitch had. The first time had brought back a sense memory so strong that she'd almost passed out. Now with her back against the wall and his hands at her throat, she knew how to break his grip. She whipped her arm across, pulling his arms out of the way. Her elbow, poised to strike, connected with his face. Her knee came up as his head fell.

"So how do you win?"

Last week she'd muttered her answer, tentatively.

"I attack," she declared.

They had stood facing each other; hands up. His hands nearly twice the size of hers and stretched far above her. With their hands alone, they had tried to knock each other off balance. It took Slim twenty, maybe twenty-five, tries to make him stumble backward.

"And what do you do after you attack?" he asked.

"Nothing," Slim said.

"Why nothing?"

"Because I never stop attacking!"

She was seated on a mat, staring straight ahead; her face was impassive, her breathing deep, easy, rhythmic. The instructor was seated just behind her.

"One last thing. The hardest lesson: we can't control the universe."

His words surprised her. For a second, her intense look flickered.

He had gotten up and was moving slowly, circling her very, very slowly. "Suddenly his maid enters. You're distracted for an instant, and he hits you—"

"That's not possible," Slim said.

He was facing her now. "To win, we must prepare even for the impossible."

Slim stared at him, not liking what she was hearing. It contradicted everything she'd worked for.

"We bend the universe to our will," he continued, "but it will only go so far."

She thought she knew what he meant. What if . . . what if Mitch did catch her off guard, get her off balance, knocked her down? What if she had to go on the defensive instead of being on the offensive, which she'd practiced all these weeks?

"So you're saying. . . ?" she started to ask.

He nodded, "Yes," and patted the mat, signaling her to lie down.

Reluctantly, she did.

"You're down," he said. "Lying here. Seemingly beaten." He ran his hand down her face, forcing her to close her eyes. "But hear me. Hold onto my voice."

As she nodded, almost imperceptibly, he stood up. "He's standing over you, he thinks he's won. . . and as sure as he's a coward, he'll try to kick you."

"Yes," she responded softly.

"And because you know what he'll do, you're smiling inside."

Her face was blank, her eyes still closed, but something had changed. As the instructor drew back his foot as if to kick her, her confidence and serenity returned.

DRESSED TO

KILL

O ut of her sweats and impeccably
dressed, Slim strode through the loft
into Jupiter's office.

He was standing at his desk. "Hey," he greeted her, looking up. "You're a different person."

"So?" It was hard to switch gears. She'd been
fighting for so long. Not just in the gym, either,
she realized. She'd been on the defensive, one
way or another, for most of her life.

"How's that guy I set you up with?"

"Good," Slim said.

"He teach you how to think?"

It was not the question she'd expected. It was more interesting and complicated. "I hope so," she answered, and before he could say more, she asked, "Did you find Mitch?"

Jupiter nodded and handed her a piece of paper. "He's sold the house. Got himself a loft down near the Marina."

"Marina Del Rey." Slim nodded, folded the paper, put it in her purse.

"How you making out with Alex?"

She looked at her watch. "I'll know in twenty-five minutes. Also, I need a woman who looks like me," she said, realizing that Jupiter was right, she was a different person, she sounded like one even to herself. Demanding, unapologetic, all business. She wasn't sure she liked it, but it would definitely serve her purpose for now. "An off-duty cop or something. Five feet four inches, one hundred ten pounds. Hair like mine but cut higher, and she should wear dark slacks and white Nikes."

She handed him a key. "I got her a room at the Washington Square Inn."

Jupiter was impressed. "What's she for?"

Reluctantly, Slim explained. "I need Mitch to think I'm here in San Francisco. Have her meet me, 5:45, top floor of Vesuvio's book-store."

"Tonight?" He scratched his handsome head, faking a frown. "That's awful short notice. I don't know if I can—"

"What?!" Slim said, "I thought Jupiter was, like, all-powerful, king of the Gods?" She turned to go. Then looked over her shoulder at him. "Oh yeah. One more thing. At some point . . . not right now because it'd be phony . . . I need you to acknowledge that I'm your kid."

She walked away without seeing the grin on his face, but sure it was there nonetheless.

● ● ●

Next stop. An electronics store. Slim had a shopping list in her purse. The final buy was the most expensive. "Are you sure this'll work?" she asked the clerk, handing over her credit card.

"You bet your life," he said, processing her bill.

Slim looked at him, then signed the slip. "Thanks, I will," she told him, as he handed her the merchandise in a distinctive red bag.

She took a cab to the pier and called L.A. from a pay phone.

"Hiller residence," the butler answered.

"Yes. Tony. Could you please tell Mrs. Hiller that I'll call her around four this afternoon?"

"Of course, Miss Slim," he said. "My pleasure."

She turned away from the phone and saw him waiting, watching her. A short guy in his late twenties, built like a fireplug, wearing a dark sweater, jeans, and a wool cap. He looked like either a sailor or a thug. *What you saw was what you got,* Slim thought, waving at him. "Alex," she nodded.

He walked over and said in his affable English accent, "Today, hon, you graduate."

They drove into downtown San Francisco and parked across the street from a strip joint.

"It's closed?" Slim asked, apprehensively.

"Till six, eh?" He hopped out of his car and came around to open her door.

She was staring at the place. "And I'd guess whoever owns it isn't a very nice person," she remarked, as he helped her out.

"That's a safe one," Alex agreed.

They crossed the street together and walked toward the shop. "Why here?" Slim asked.

"You've got soft hands, you've worked hard," he said, "The tricky part now is controlling your nerves." It was a bit different from fighting, Alex had assured her, took a different set of nerves. Still she could bring what she'd learned to bear:

the concentration, the breathing, the single-mindedness.

When they reached the entryway, Slim knew why he'd chosen the place, and why in broad daylight. "You mean the people on the street," she said, taking out her tools.

"Today it's people on the street, tomorrow it's him," Alex agreed. "You gotta go in when the alarm's off, meaning he's inside, he could be awake—"

"I'm aware, okay?" Slim said, eyeing the security lock. "Let's do it."

Alex moved slightly to block the view as Slim bent over and slipped a tool into the device. She worked quietly, focusing intently, yet trying to stay aware of everything around her. Alex was keeping a casual lookout. He wouldn't be at Mitch's place.

She sensed something, thought she heard someone coming, just as Alex said, "We got company, doll."

Slim kept going on the lock.

"Forget it," Alex said, "You're too slow."

Slim opened the door. Alex glanced down, nodded. She closed the door again and stood up, just as a rough looking guy, who could've been the owner for all they knew, called out, "Hey. What're you up to?"

Slim stared at him, her face hard. "We were hoping to see some action," she said, "but it looks like they're closed."

He didn't believe them. He stared back at her. Alex took her arm and they strolled off down the block, knowing the guy was watching them. By the time they got to the corner, he'd given up and gone looking for new trouble somewhere else. Alex whistled. "That's what I call graduation under pressure."

Grinning, Slim said, "Think I'll celebrate."

●　●　●

Waiting for her manicure, Slim sat in a chair, her freshly shampooed hair wrapped in a towel, cell phone at her ear. She was talking with Mitch's mother.

"And where is Gracie?" Mrs. Hiller asked, as Slim knew she would. She couldn't have scripted it better herself.

"She's coming day after tomorrow, then we're flying to L.A. I was thinking, after the hearing, maybe I could bring her by."

"Tell me something," Mitch's mother asked. "Why is this call different? You were always worried about how long we talked."

"That was when I was out in the country, Mrs.

H. I'm in a big city now, meeting with my lawyer, so there're lots of cell phones—"

Something outside caught her eye. She looked out the window of the beauty salon at the car that had just pulled up across the street. A man in a leather jacket got out. He was peering at the shop and talking on a cell phone.

"You wouldn't believe how many," Slim said. "Don't worry. No one can trace this."

He was back in his car when she exited the beauty salon wearing a pale trenchcoat with her black pants and white Nikes. Leather man waited a few seconds, then got out of his car and followed her. Slim walked hurriedly, then swerved into Vesuvio's bookstore.

He saw her and hesitated, unsure of whether to go in after her or not. He decided to wait outside. Keeping an eye on the bookstore, he flipped open his cell phone and made a call. He'd barely said hello, when the pale coat and white Nikes came out. The man snapped his phone shut and followed her.

Slim exited the bookstore without her coat, a few minutes later, and headed in the other direction. She was ready. She was gone.

ENOUGH

For a long time, Slim watched the lights reflected in the water. They were mostly streetlights. Almost all the windows of the stylish converted warehouses that lined the marina were dark.

Mitch's windows were dark.

She had counted up from the bottom floor, down from the top, and over from each side of the soaring brick building. But she didn't really need to. They were his windows and he was inside. She'd seen him going up the outside stairs and unlocking the door three hours ago. It wasn't easy with the blonde hanging off him, but good old Mitch was always good with his hands.

She'd seen his bedroom lights go on and then go off and then go on again briefly when either Mitch or the blonde had gone into the kitchen. The lights, all of them, had been off for at least an hour now.

Slim set down her yellow duffel bag. It was heavy, almost as full as her head. Every item inside the bag matched five or six things she had to remember. She checked her watch again. It was a minute later than the last time she'd looked. "Let's do it," she murmured, stretching her neck, her arms.

Unzipping the duffel, she pulled out the set of tools Alex had given her. He'd have been proud of her, too. She had the front door unlocked in five minutes flat.

Even with the architectural plans she'd gotten off the net, the apartment setup was complicated. And very Mitch. Soaring concrete walls, metal beams, odd shaped alcoves, hidden niches, balconies fit for a tyrant, and high tech devices for every occasion.

The entrance hall itself was bizarre, opening onto a mezzanine balcony midway between the

sunken kitchen and the high-ceilinged bedroom suite. Opposite the front door was a key-
pad alarm device. Its green light glowed in the
dark, indicating that the system was turned on.
It took Slim longer to disarm the hall alarm, but
she did it, and then crept up to a narrow loft
braced by rafters from which she could look
down at the room in which Mitch was sleeping.

He stirred as she set down the duffel.

He sat up, frowning, dazed, cocked his head,
and listened.

Above him, Slim went cold, kept still. But
Mitch had heard something, some faint movement in the silence. He got up to investigate.

From her corner, Slim watched him, surprised
at how vulnerable he looked in his boxer shorts.
She had grown used to the instructor's height
and muscular massiveness. Automatically, almost
objectively, she observed Mitch, sizing him up,
seeking out weaknesses, realizing suddenly, that
she had become the stalker.

Hearing nothing more, he got back into bed.
The young girl next to him turned over, muttered something, then went back to sleep. Mitch
didn't. He lay there with his eyes open, staying
very still, listening.

• • •

The apartment was flooded with daylight. Slim smelled coffee. Looking down, she saw Mitch in the kitchen, dressed for work, sipping coffee. The blonde came in and he offered her some. She said she had to get home and change for work. Mitch nodded, unconcerned. "I'll call you," he said, barely looking up.

The girl stared at him a second. "You want my number?" she asked.

"Sure." Without glancing at it, he took the paper on which she'd scribbled her number. "Thanks for everything," he said.

"Yeah. You, too," the young blonde answered, sarcastically. "I really appreciate it." She let herself out.

Mitch poured himself another coffee and dialed a number on his cell phone. "Lucy? Hey," he said. "Yeah, I was working late."

Even though he was using his saccharine voice, Slim could hear his words. She could remember them, too, and the sticky sweet sincerity she'd craved.

"Tonight's no good either," Mitch said. "I've got a morning flight to San Francisco."

In the rafters, Slim listened intently.

"If it was pleasure, you'd be going too. No, I'm going to get my daughter."

She held still, held her eyes, her mouth still,

didn't allow herself a gasp or a knowing smile.

"Sure, the custody hearing's here next week," Mitch was telling Lucy, "but it looks like Gracie's being brought to San Francisco and Slim, my ex-wife . . . well, seems like she completely vanished."

His words echoed his threats when he was trying to strangle her in her hallway. But now he said it without rancor, almost as if he were sorry. Poor ex-wife Slim.

"Right off the face of the earth. I doubt they'll ever find her this time."

Slim's jaw tightened. The lawyer's words resonated in her mind: *The custody hearing? It's a way to find you. And he can come to wherever you are . . . and kill you.*

He was packing his briefcase now, holding the phone between his neck and shoulder. "Oh, sure, baby. Yeah, I want her to meet *you*. We'll call when we get in." He lowered his voice, his lulling, seductive voice, "You too," he said, and clicked off.

Finally, he headed for the door. Slim waited until he set the alarm system and it beeped. She waited until the front door opened and shut, and then gave him two minutes more, just to be sure, before she climbed down and began to check out the kitchen.

He'd left his coffee machine on. Slim hesitated, then shut it off. She'd opened the fridge looking for something to eat when she heard the alarm beep again. A key twisted in the lock.

Mitch was back.

Slim dropped silently to the floor behind the kitchen island. She could hear Mitch's footsteps approaching. They grew louder. She covered her mouth and slipped around the edge of the counter just as he walked into the kitchen—heading straight for the coffee machine.

He looked at it and frowned. Hadn't he left it on? He listened again, and turned to look at the exact spot where she'd been crouched a moment before.

Slim sat backed up against the side of the island and prayed he couldn't hear her heart racing. *Don't take one more step,* she silently begged. *Just go. Please.* All her training, all her plans would be worth nothing if he found her out at this moment, huddled on the floor in his kitchen. Out of the corner of her eye, she spotted her yellow duffel bag on a nearby ledge. She hoped Mitch couldn't see it from where he stood. *LEAVE!* She willed telepathically.

After what seemed like the longest thirty seconds of Slim's life, Mitch glanced at his watch and hurried out, stopping only to reset the security alarm.

This time, she watched his car pull away. Then she breathed a deep sigh of relief, poured herself a cup of coffee and speed-dialed her cell phone. "I'm in," she told Ginny.

● ● ●

Before anything else, she focused on her breathing. When it was steady again, when oxygen flowed smoothly to her brain, Slim retrieved her duffel bag and got to work.

She checked the phone line. Following it to the place where it entered the apartment, she disconnected it. She found the electrical box, opened it and found the main switch. Rifling through the kitchen drawers, she removed every knife she could find and dumped them into the vegetable crisper in the fridge.

She got the metal detector out of her duffel and found the gun in his night-table drawer. She took it out and tossed it into a clothes hamper. Where the gun had been, she left several handwritten letters.

Dear Mitch, Thanks for letting me come talk about Gracie. I'm glad you're willing to admit your temper,

and—let's not mince words—the physical abuse you
subjected me to.

Perhaps with your new attitude, we can really work
something out. Per your last letter, I'll see you the
evening of . . .

The metal detector went off again around
Mitch's desk. After searching the area, she
found a second gun in a secret compartment
hidden behind a false front, and, to her surprise, an old picture of the two of them. *Slim
and Mitch*, she shook her head, ripping up the
picture. She threw both the shreds and the gun
into a box full of rolled-up blueprints.

She walked the apartment, familiarizing herself with every inch of it. She looked from
one piece of furniture to another, back and
forth, gauging the distances between them.
Occasionally, she moved something slightly,
after assessing her fighting spaces and angles.

She fixed herself a snack from his fridge,
stared out the back windows at the Pacific, then
took the red bag from the electronics store out
of the duffel. There was a machine inside. She
plugged it in, tucked it behind the couch, and
put her cell phone beside it. She dialed Ginny's
number. After a few rings, the phone cut off.
Signal faded, the message read. *Call lost.*

At three o'clock, she changed into a black leotard and sweatpants. She took off her cloth shoes and laced up her black steel-toed work-boots. Sitting at the edge of Mitch's bed, she studied the balustrade separating the sleeping loft from the living room below, calculating the space between the rails and the length of the drop. Then she continued getting ready, slipped gaudy rings onto her fingers, chunky rings with large-faceted stones and ornate designs, and bound each hand tightly with black tape.

At four, she made one last check: every wall, surface, every drawer. With her eyes closed, she walked the space again. Backing up, moving with ease and grace, sliding deftly to the side as she approached a couch, desk, chair. She knew where every piece of furniture was and how to navigate around it. Finally, she rubbed a thin layer of Vaseline all over her face and neck. She wanted to be slippery if he tried to grab her—he might be stronger, but she would be smarter and quicker. That was what counted in this match.

As the light dimmed outside, she stopped and stood perfectly still for a long moment, poised like an animal in the forest. She glanced at the chair facing the front door, measuring it in her mind, deciding. Then she walked behind the couch, turned off the machine, and auto-dialed her cell phone.

"Hey," Ginny answered. "You okay?"

"Gin, say it again," Slim asked, softly.

"Say what?"

"You know. What you told me."

"Okay," Ginny said. "You have a divine animal right to protect your own life and the life of your offspring."

Slim let it in. "Yeah," she said. "Thanks." She hung up and turned the machine back on and stashed away her cell phone. Then she lowered herself into the chair facing the door and waited in the fading light.

• • •

Fifteen minutes, twenty. She heard his footsteps on the stairs outside, heard him punch in his alarm code. The hair on the back of her neck bristled. That was all. She continued breathing evenly, moved more like a tepid breeze than a person.

Mitch came in, turned on the light, and walked toward the bedroom. He had just taken off his jacket when the power went out. He froze, a silhouette in the darkness. Looking out the window, he saw lights on in the neighboring buildings.

He cocked his head, listened, and heard nothing. Cautiously, he walked to the door of the bedroom, stopped, waited there, then took two more steps.

"It's me," Slim said.

He nodded slowly in the dark. "Yeah," he answered, "I thought so." Looking around, he made his way quietly to the bed, to the night table where Slim had found the pistol. He tried to cover his movements by talking. "This morning, too?"

"You always forget to turn off the coffee." Slim's eyes had adjusted to the darkness. She could see now almost as well as if the lights were on. But she didn't need to. Her ears picked up every nuance. She could find him, the disturbance in the space she'd studied, with her eyes shut.

He was rummaging in the drawer. Slim heard the rustle of papers, the letters she had put there. "I found it, Mitch," she told him.

He picked up the phone, listened, heard no dial tone. Squinting in the darkness, moving back to the chair where he'd tossed his jacket, he fished out his cell phone. The dial glowed as he punched in 9-1-1 and pressed SEND. The dial went dark, then blinked back on. Mitch stared at it, tried again. Again it went dead.

"It's a machine," Slim said, startling him this time. "Knocks out cell phones."

He threw the phone down and walked out of the bedroom. Looking for her in the vast space, with its dim slanting light and dense shadows, he went toward his desk.

"I found that gun, too," she said.

It stopped Mitch cold. He didn't know where to go or what to do.

"Scared?" Slim asked.

His laugh was dry, contemptuous. "Of what?"

"Now is when you decide, Mitch. Whether you're a coward. If you are, you can run. I won't stop you."

"You going to shoot me with my own guns?" he said.

"I threw them away."

"Then someone's here with you." It was a statement, not a question.

"No," Slim said quietly.

"You're alone? No way," he decided.

"Why not?"

The lights came back on. He saw her and was startled at first, then relieved. She was small, slight, a nothing. She held nothing. He leaned back against a low dresser, reassured by the sight of her. She'd grown in the darkness, in his imagination. Now she was right-sized again.

She came away from the power box and started up the stairs toward him. "This is what you wanted, right? What you were going to San Francisco for. The chance to get me alone?"

She faced him, crouching slightly, her taped hands apart, her feet planted in an attack stance. Mitch gave a short laugh and stared at her in disbelief. "You want to fight me man-to-man?"

"Woman, Mitch," she said.

"Yeah, that's what I mean." It was ludicrous. "Man against woman. You sure that's fair?"

"Fair to who?" Slim asked.

He laughed.

She moved toward him. Finally, he stood, towering over her. "No, I'm sorry," he said, utterly at ease, as if having a casual conversation. "I can't do this."

"Can't do what?" She lunged and slapped his face.

He touched his cheek where her open hand had landed. "This is ridiculous."

"You could hit me before, couldn't you?" Slim goaded him. "When I was defenseless." She slapped him again, harder.

He looked at her, smiled, shook his head. "That's not going to—"

She landed another one, this time with her fist. And this time, Mitch's smile looked a little forced through his clenched teeth. "Like I was saying, Slim, that's not going to do it."

"Then what will do it? Are you really such a coward that you can only hit me when I'm not expecting it?" She lunged in, jumped back before he could react, slid to the side, and slapped him again.

Mitch's jaw rippled, but he just stood there, arms down, looking at her. He shook his head casually, then started to walk away.

Slim went after him, and—BAM. He whirled on her, punching as he turned. She moved quickly so the blow landed on her shoulder. Still, it knocked her down.

"Is that enough?" Mitch asked, his relaxed stance gone.

She glared up at him. He took another step toward her and she slipped through the sleeping loft railing, dropping down, landing in the living room. He looked down at her, surprised. "More?" he asked, trying to regain his cool.

Slim gestured with her hand. *Come on . . . let's go.*

Mitch didn't like the arrogance of the gesture. His lip curled slightly as he moved down the stairs toward her. "I don't understand, Slim. How does this work for you?" he asked.

Before he hit the bottom step, she was gone, crouched in the shadows beside the fireplace.

"I mean, this is carefully thought out." He was looking for her. "But say you succeed—beat me up or whatever. You're not going to murder me . . . "

He moved in her direction. She leaped up, slugged his face.

". . . so all you've done is further piss me off," he continued. And he was pissed off. The last blow had hurt. His fists were raised, waiting to connect.

"Self-defense isn't murder," Slim said.

It stopped him cold. He lowered his hands a moment as he took in what she meant. He stared at her. "You don't have the guts."

She just looked at him.

Mitch blinked. He saw it in her eyes. She did have the guts. Okay, then. It was time to quit kidding around. He stiffened, his hands curled into fists again. But his voice stayed soft, lulling. "Come on," he said, "it's not self-defense when you break in here and attack me."

"Attack you? All I did is slap you around a little," Slim mocked.

Mitch lunged at her and missed, but he kept stalking her, kept talking, "You really think . . . you think you'll kill me and get away with it?"

"I told you," Slim said, backing away, weaving

and ducking, "Self-defense. I came here, as arranged in our letters, Mitch. To talk about Gracie—"

"Letters? What are you . . . ? There are no letters."

"Sure. In the drawer where your pistol was. You just left prints all over them, didn't you?"

He stared at her, stunned.

"You attacked me. I fought back. If necessary, I can give myself more bruises."

Who was she? What was she talking about, killing him? Suddenly he was more focused and more terrifying, backing her up, maneuvering her into a corner. "I don't care how long it takes, Slim." His voice was husky, deep. "We both know I only have to hit you once. One good hit, and it's over."

He rushed at her. She spun away, slamming him into the corner, against shelves filled with drinks and glassware. His face was nicked, bleeding. He touched the scratch, incredulous. She had drawn first blood. As he regained his balance and turned back toward her, she threw his metal audiocassette rack down in front of him. Mitch tripped over it. And fell to the ground.

Slim moved in fast, delivering her first really savage blow. Blood flowed from his nose. "He can bleed," she said, as he climbed back to his feet.

"You can count on one thing, Toots. After this, you'll never see Gracie again."

"*You* never will," she countered with unsettling assurance.

He lunged for her again. Again she evaded him. And he lost it, went berserk, threw furniture at her, scrambled over the couch, turning it over, sending it crashing down. Slim hurled whatever she could grab at him and, narrowly evading him, she ran up the stairs.

Mitch grabbed her foot. Her body knew the move, reacted fast. She kicked him in the face with her other foot. He released her. She clambered up, stood above him. "I'm confused, Mitchy. Aren't you a man? Can't you hit me again, even once?"

She had misjudged how badly he was hurt. He leaped up the stairs and raced across the space toward her. "You bitch!" He grabbed her by the shoulders and slammed her against the wall. "What do you think now?" he shouted, slamming her again. "All your training?" He was in her face, clamping her against the wall, ready to slam her head against it again. "You're screwed, honey! You're—"

She went for his eyes with her hands.

He whipped his head away, and grasped her throat. She felt his thumbs pressing against her windpipe. She'd been here before and nearly died. Only Gracie tearing at his hair had saved her.

For an instant, it seemed she would die. All she could see was the homicidal fury in Mitch's eyes.

Then her body remembered. She whipped her arm across, pulling his arms out of the way. Her elbow was poised, ready to strike.

Mitch's face showed shock at the sudden reversal.

Her elbow flew up into his face. Once! Twice! She slammed his head against her knee, and sent him flying backward. His head hit the kitchen counter. And he dropped.

Slim scrambled down the stairs after him. He was out. Lying flat on his back. His face bloodied, leering even in unconsciousness. She picked up the heavy marble cutting board from the counter and held it above him, prepared to deliver the *coup de grace*, the blow that would kill him.

Her mind raced, remembering, calling up every reason she had to finish him now. Her face was contorted in rage and confusion. Her arms trembled. She tossed down the marble tray, intentionally missing Mitch, and turned away with tears in her eyes.

Slim retrieved her cell phone, shut off the phone blocker and pressed redial. Staring out the window, she said, "I can't, Gin."

"Oh my God, you're okay. You beat him?" Ginny shrieked.

"Yeah," Slim said.

"He's dead?"

"I can't do it, Ginny."

"Slim," her friend urged, "He'll come after you."

"I know," she said.

"He'll come after Gracie!"

"I know all that!" Slim cried. "But I still can't . . . I'm not a killer, Gin."

A shadow rose over her head. She felt it before she saw it. "I'm not him," she said, turning instinctively, trying to see what was behind her.

It was Mitch. His face was crazed and bloody. He was holding a wooden lamp with both hands. Holding it high above her. It was meant to land flush on her skull. It came down on the side of her head, because she had turned.

Still, the blow sent her crashing to the floor.

"Hello?" Ginny's voice cried from the dropped cell phone. "Slim? You there?"

Mitch stood over Slim, dazed, bloody, beaten, but triumphant. The lamp moved in his hands. He was rotating it, menacingly. Preparing to hit her again.

"Oh God. Should I call the cops? Answer me!"

The voice distracted Mitch. He picked up the phone. "Listen to me, bitch," he rasped. Ginny went silent. "If you value your children, don't call anybody. It's over, okay? It's all over."

He threw the phone onto the overturned couch and moved back toward Slim.

She hadn't moved. But the shock, the fear, that had contorted her features, were gone.

As sure as he's a coward, he will try to kick you. Hold onto my voice. You're ready.

Mitch saw the hint of a smile on her face. He couldn't believe it. Overcome with rage, he pulled back his foot—

Slim's eyes opened, just a slit.

His foot swung forward.

Her legs grabbed his, and twisted him down.

Mitch fell.

And what do you do to win?

I attack.

And what do you do after you attack.

Nothing.

Slim leaped up and hit him, closed fisted, again and again. Her blows so complete, so full out, that the rings under the black tape jarred her hands even as they intensified each blow.

I never stop attacking.

Slim thought about the night she caught Darcelle on the line, how nonchalant Mitch was. She felt all the times he had punched her, the pain of her bruises. She saw little Gracie's face the night Mitch had thrown her down in his rage to kill. He didn't care about them. He'd never cared about anyone. All those sudden, fierce memories channeled an adrenaline rush Slim didn't know she was capable of.

Her last hit sent Mitch flying over the railing. He crashed down onto the glass table below. His neck snapped. His head lay at an awkward angle, a position impossible for a living man.

Slim stared down at him in disbelief.

• • •

She heard the sirens, far off. The first police car skidded to a halt in front of her seven minutes later. Slim was sitting on the wall outside Marina del Rey, waiting for them.

She had dropped the cell phone into the water. Then the duffel. She watched as they sank. Now the revolving light of the police car rotated red and blue across her battered and bloodied face.

Two cops came out of their car, guns drawn, and approached her. "Some woman called. Ginny. You're her friend?"

Slim nodded her head.

"He's still in there?" the younger one asked.

She nodded again.

"Armed? Dangerous?"

Slowly Slim shook her head. He studied her face, flinching at the bruises, as his partner went inside.

"Looks like you're one of the lucky ones," the cop said, as Slim lowered her head and started to cry.

• • •

Slim was at LAX an hour early. Where was her concentration and balance now? She looked down and realized that she was actually wringing her hands. She wished she could wring her mind instead. It was awash with uncertainty and unanswered questions.

Would Gracie be all right, happy to see her, still fearful and angry?

Ginny had assured Slim that Gracie was flourishing in the Hawaiian sunshine and that, as promised, she could dribble a basketball behind her back. Well, one out of five tries anyway.

Still Slim remembered their goodbye. Gracie's unalterable sadness. Her expressionless face, her wriggling out of Slim's arms, not wanting to be hugged, or even touched.

Passengers began to disembark, waving, calling to friends, pouring into the waiting area. The colors of their holiday outfits seemed almost painfully bright. She felt as though she'd been living in a cave. Her eyes were having trouble adjusting to light, to the possibilities of a life unshadowed by fear.

She saw Ginny first, her red blouse, her arm up and waving. And then there, at knee level, walking in front of Ginny was Gracie, chattering amiably with Ginny's little girl. A purple flight bag was draped across her small torso; her hair, in two ponytails, fastened by bright barrettes.

"Gracie," Slim called, waving like mad, jumping up and down so that her daughter could see her.

Gracie turned. Slim saw Ginny put a hand on her own children's shoulders, holding them back, as Gracie screamed, "Mommy, Mommy!" and ran toward Slim, weaving through the crowd that flowed between them.

Gracie pulled off the little purple flight bag, threw it down. "Mommy, I've got stuff to show you from Hawaii," she shrieked, then leaped into Slim's outstretched arms and clung there, arms, legs, cheek pressed tight, blissfully binding them. "Mommy, Mommy, where are we going next?"

Slim laughed. Over Gracie's shoulder, she saw Ginny's teary-eyed joyfulness. "Anywhere you want," she promised.

"Emerald City," Gracie whispered in Slim's ear.

Slim swallowed back a surge of emotion. She flashed a smile larger than any she'd dared before.

"That's where I was thinking, too."